MW00652750

christmas

July

Merry Christmas
2004

WARNING

You are about to embark on an adventure unlike any you've had before. Reading this book is like taking a wild vacation—you begin each day the same, but you end with a totally new and different story every time you read.

As you go through this book, you'll notice that the action stops just when something exciting is about to happen. You then have to make a choice about what you want to do next. Choose one option and turn to the appropriate page. Continue reading and choosing, creating your own adventure story right up to the exciting finish.

Read the book over and over, choosing a different ending each time. Try following a new track each day and see how many different adventures you can have with just one book. A thrilling vacation in Tanzania is waiting for you; start reading today!

EAST AFRICAN ADVENTURES

The
Hunting
Safari

by T.J. Matthews

illustrations by Judy Rheberg

Wycliffe
Partners in Bible Translation

Orlando, Florida
1-800-WYCLIFFE
www.wycliffe.org

You Choose: East African Adventures
The Hunting Safari
© 2003 Wycliffe Bible Translators
P.O. Box 628200
Orlando, FL 32862-8200

ISBN 0-938978-34-9

Printed in the United States of America

Visit Wycliffe's Web site at *www.wycliffe.org*

To order additional copies of *The Hunting Safari*, contact Wycliffe's Media Resource Center, 1-800-992-5433, *media_resource_center @wycliffe.org*

Dedicated to the Salowitz family
Steve, Kim, Jacob, Jeffrey, Joseph
and their dog, Simba.

ACKNOWLEDGMENTS

I would like to thank Jesus Christ—for saving me by grace, for giving me the opportunity to write and adventures to write about. I would like to thank all the Kahunda missionary kids—Salowitzes, Hamiltons, Luckeys and Milligans, who shared their lives in Kahunda with me.

Mom and Dad, your consistent encouragement is invaluable. Cliff, thank you for being a wonderful brother—you're the reason I can write about siblings who get along and who love each other. To my African friend Hilda—it was your friendship that enabled me to master the language of Kiswahili and that opened the door to East Africa. I look forward to a day in heaven when we can speak to each other freely without any language barriers.

I would like to thank Dorothea Landers, Carol Dowsett, and Pixie Christensen for encouraging me in the early stages of writing. I would like to thank my teachers—Bridget Howard and John and Glenda Leonard—who all worked with me and encouraged me while the books were in progress. I would also like to thank my colleagues Carol Cruzen, Heather Pubols and Judy Rheberg for seeing this project through to its completion.

And finally, *To Him who is able to keep you from falling and to present you before His glorious presence without fault and with great joy—to the only God our Savior be glory, majesty, power and authority, through Jesus Christ our Lord, before all ages, now and forevermore! Amen.* Jude 1:24–25 (NIV)

—T.J. Matthews

PREFACE

Dear Reader,

Once upon a time a family moved from the United States of America to a village in Tanzania called Kahunda. There were two children in this family, a boy and a girl, who spent their early years living out many of the African adventures you are about to read.

As you may have already guessed, I was one of the children in this family. When I eventually left my village home at age 13, I remembered the adventures from my life in Kahunda and from the other missionary kids who lived there at various times. Kahunda is still a part of me, and so I have written the book you are about to read.

—T.J. Matthews

THE EAST AFRICAN SAFARIS

Two of your best friends, David and Danielle, moved to Africa about three years ago. Dave is older than Danielle, with short blond hair and blue eyes. Danielle is a black-eyed brunette with long curly hair. You have been emailing them and hearing all about their village in Tanzania where people bathe in Lake Victoria, deal with African wildlife and don't speak English. This summer they have invited you to visit them in their village, and your parents have agreed! As you board the airplane, you look fondly at your own country, secretly wondering if you will ever see it again. It's a jungle out there, right? Anything could happen.

After two nine-hour flights with a stop in London, your plane lands on a runway in the huge city of Nairobi, Kenya. In the shove of passengers leaving the plane, you spot Dave and Danielle with their parents, "Uncle" Darryl and "Aunt" Debbie, waiting for you. As you all walk to get your luggage through tight airport hallways, Danielle turns to you. "We'll stay in Nairobi for a couple of days until you get over your jet lag. Then we'll fly out to the village. If you have anything you want to find on the Internet, you'd better do it now 'cause this is your last chance. There are no phone connections in Kahunda."

"Think you'll be ready for it?" Dave asks, with a slightly joking tone. You nod.

A few days later you leave the big city on a six-seater plane. Before take-off, the pilot makes sure that everyone has a seat belt on and points out the vomit bags. You notice that Uncle Darryl keeps one ready.

You arrive in the Mwanza airport, step out of the plane straight onto the tarmac and carry your luggage from the runway over to the airport's waiting room. In Nairobi most signs were in English. Now everything is in Kiswahili. Uncle Darryl and Aunt Debbie don't seem to have any trouble making the switch.

As you all sit in the waiting room on comfortable couches drinking bottled sodas, you decide to ask the question that has been on your mind since their family moved to Africa three years before. "Why did you all move to Africa? I know that you're missionaries, but what exactly do you do?"

Uncle Darryl answers, "We're missionaries with Wycliffe Bible Translators. The goal of the organization is to see all people able to read the Bible in their first language, also called their heart language. Many people groups speak languages that haven't been written yet. Wycliffe helps people develop alphabets and dictionaries to record their culture as well as to translate the Bible into their language. We came to work with the Wazinza people. Right now I'm working with five Wazinza translators to translate the book of Genesis into their language, Kizinza."

Aunt Debbie continues, "The Wazinza are a people group scattered around this area. If you include all the Kizinza dialects, the group probably numbers about 250,000 people. Though most of them can speak Kiswahili (the national language of Tanzania), the Kiswahili Bible generally doesn't interest them; but now that Wazinza translators are working to translate the Bible into their language, the Wazinza are very interested. We've heard of nursery schools that have just started teaching Wazinza children the Zinza alphabet. Once the children get into primary school, they'll learn to read and write the national language, Kiswahili, but they'll get a reading background in their first language first."

"Hey! The DC-3 is landing!" Dave calls from the door of the waiting room, looking out to the runway. You and Danielle get up to go look.

"Is that the plane we'll be taking to Kahunda?" you ask, surprised. It could probably hold 20 people.

"No, we'll be taking another six-seater Cessna," Dave informs you. You return your bottles to the refreshment counter and then board your flight to the village.

You fly over the coast of Lake Victoria, looking down at farmland sprinkled with mud house compounds. Thirty minutes later the six-seater airplane bumps down on a grassy lakeside airstrip and taxis to a stop. You look at the crowd of people around the plane. Some are smiling, some frown. You wonder why they are all staring at you.

"Danny, these people are looking at me like I'm a space alien; what's up with this?"

"Well, you are a space alien." She laughs at your puzzled face and explains. "These people have lived in this village and the surrounding ones all of their lives. Many have never been to a city. You're a weird foreigner when you are here, and people stare at you just because you're different and because a novelty is always worth looking at."

A three-minute walk along the lake from the airstrip takes you to Dave and Danielle's house. Uncle Darryl brings the luggage in the truck. After a two-minute drive from the airstrip, you arrive at their brick house. Lake Victoria starts about 40 feet from the house. It then stretches out as far away as you can see. "The bricks are made of cement and termite sand," Dave tells you.

The house has a grass roof built about two feet over a metal one. "The grass roof is to keep the house cool in the hot weather and to dampen the loud sound of rain beating on metal," Danielle explains. "When it rains on the metal roof at church, you can't hear the speaker!"

"After you move in, I was thinking we could go on a quick hunting trip," says Dave. "I have an extra slingshot."

(Go to page 6)

"Remember, be home by 5:30!" Aunt Debbie calls as you and Dave walk out the back door.

"Okay, Mom," Dave replies, curling the brim of his baseball cap and giving it a final tug down over his eyes. The two of you cross the backyard and enter the brush behind it. It is sunny; the bush is full of scrubby bushes, gnarly trees and lots of birds. "I'm sure glad you decided to come with me," says Dave, pushing aside all the branches in his way, which swing back after him, hitting you in the face. "Danny will sulk at home for a while, but she'll be okay." Dave has equipped you with a Y-shaped slingshot with a rubber strap tied between the two ends of the Y. He has also prepared you with a pocketful of small rocks. "Our family rule about hunting," he explains, "is that you only hunt what will be eaten by you or your pets."

The air is dry and the sun is hot. A fish eagle screeches overhead. You enter a small, sandy clearing. Some African boys are standing around inside it. Dave greets them in Kiswahili, the national language. They are all smaller than Dave and wearing ragged play-clothes. They are all out hunting with their slingshots too.

So far, all the birds that you have seen have been small. Dave shoots at some of them but without much interest. He's a fairly good shot, though. His rocks normally fly within a foot of the bird. "I've been shooting slingshots since I got here," Dave tells you. "A small bird is an accomplishment; they're hard to hit. You don't get much meat from one, though." He shoots at a sunbird in a nearby tree, misses and then goes to find his rock.

Looking out through the branches of the scrub tree under which Dave is busily combing the ground, you spot a large dark spot on top of a far-off tree. A closer examination reveals it to be a large bird. It must be a foot and a half long! It has a long beak and mostly brown feathers with a few glossy green ones on its wings.

(If you decide to shoot your slingshot at the bird, go to page 8.)
(If you tell Dave about it, go to page 9.)
(If you ignore it, go to page 11.)

You pull a rock out of your pocket and place it into the leather patch in the middle of the rubber strips coming from the ends of your slingshot.

(If you are good at using a slingshot, go to page 15.)
(If you have used one before but are not very skilled at it, go to page 18.)
(If you have never used a slingshot before, go to page 20.)

"Dave, look, there's a really big bird up there!"

"Where?" Dave looks up excitedly.

"There!"

Dave looks at the nearby tree in the direction you're pointing and frowns. "I don't see anything."

"No, farther back. On that tall tree."

"Aha! Good, good." Dave pulls out his slingshot and carefully takes aim.

A rock whizzes past your ear. Off in the distance, you watch as the bird is knocked off the branch. It gives a hoarse cry. You hear branches breaking and a soft plop as it hits the ground.

"*Wewe!*" Dave glares at the triumphant African boy standing behind him, slingshot in hand. "*Ume iba ndege yangu!*"

"*Sasa ndege ni yangu. Unahitagi kupiga ndege yako haraka zaidi!*"

As the boy runs off grinning to find his quarry, you ask Dave what they said.

"I said, 'Hey, whatcha doing, man? You just stole my bird!' and he said it was his bird because I wasn't fast enough."

The boy walks by carrying his bird and says something to Dave in Kiswahili.

"What did he say?" you want to know.

"Nothing," Dave answers, looking insulted.

"Come on, what did he say?"

"Okay, he said he was doing the world a favor by shooting that bird because I would have missed it."

Dave yells something after the leaving boy. He returns, eyes Dave coolly and then makes a proposition.

"What did he say?"

"He's offering me, 'The Shooting Challenge,'" says Dave, looking puzzled.

"What's that?"

"I have no idea."

(If you want him to accept the challenge, go to page 33.)
(If you would rather continue hunting somewhere else, go to page 36.)

"You know," says Dave, as you leave the clearing and keep walking along through the brush, "I haven't seen anything worth shooting yet. There are little birds everywhere, but they would hardly be enough to feed my cat, much less me." Dave keeps walking and then stops mid-step. You look at the ground. A baby bird lies quaking and peeping in a small hollow of sand where Dave was about to step.

"Well, little guy," says Dave, picking up the baby bird, who immediately perches on his thumb, "you wouldn't be meal enough for a kitten." The bird quakes in fear and holds tightly onto Dave's finger.

"Here," says Dave, handing the bird to you, "I'm going to look for his nest. Something will get him if we leave him lying on the ground, anything from bugs to wild dogs. There is a story that if you touch a baby bird that has fallen out of its nest, its mother won't go near it. I don't believe that. But even if it's true, the bird has a better chance of survival in its nest than on the ground." He catches himself. "We'll shoot it someday."

The bird is using its tiny clawed feet to stand on your index finger. It has stopped shaking and looks up at you with a quizzical expression.

"Aha!" says Dave looking straight up into a tree nearby. "There it is! And that bird must be the mother right up there." Sure enough, a bigger bird is flying toward the nest. All of a sudden it dive-bombs, coming straight for you. You duck just in time.

"Give me the baby bird, quick!" Dave says in a loud whisper. He cups his hand around the peeping baby bird and then races to the tree and begins a precarious one-handed climb toward the nest. The mother bird dives. "Yeeeeooooowww!" yells Dave, in pain. The mother bird climbs skyward and gets ready for another torpedo hit. She shoots downward. "Help!" yells Dave. With one hand holding onto the tree and the other holding onto the baby bird, he is unable to defend himself.

Another hit sends Dave scrambling up the tree full speed. He reaches the nest at the top of the tree, about 11 feet off the ground, puts the little bird neatly in the nest and turns to face the mother bird who has risen for another strike. "See? I put your little bird back; you can stop now. Ahhhhhhhhhhhhhhhhhhh!" The bird attacks. Dave begins swinging his arms at the bird as she hits him full in the stomach. Dave reaches for something to grab onto but falls off his branch. He catches it on the way down and hangs there, his feet six feet above the ground, with nothing below except rough underbrush. The bird begins descending rapidly, heading for his right armpit. In a fleeting moment Dave looks at the bird, then at the ground, then at you. He gives you a mournful look and then drops. The bird sails harmlessly above his head as he goes down, down, and then crash-rolls across the terrain. He gets up, brushing off the leaves and sandy dirt and rubbing the sore place on his back where he landed on a small stump.

"Always remember when you fall, to relax, and then roll when you hit the ground. That way you won't break any bones." Dave is always ready with a lesson or advice, even in the most perilous of circumstances.

The bird is heading for you, beak first. You and Dave tear off through the undergrowth, getting stabbed by the half-inch-long beak. About 100 feet away, the bird gives up chase. You and Dave both have rips in your clothes, not to mention a few scratches on your arms and legs.

"You know something? I've had enough hunting for the day," says Dave, looking at a hole in his shirt. "We don't have to go home yet, though. In another part of the woods there are big trees with vines hanging off them. The trees are perfect for climbing. There are also some large pits dug into the sand from when people tried to mine and sell the sand a while back. Those are fun too. We have this one root sticking out over one of them that we call the diving board."

(If you want to go climb trees, go to page 58.)
(If you want to go to the sandpits, go to page 64.)

You check the rock you took out of your pocket. It's long and narrow. Bad choice. You pull a handful of rocks out of your pocket and find a rounder one. You may only get one shot at this, so you want the rock you use to be symmetrical. You fit the chosen rock into your slingshot and hold up the Y of the tool so that the bird is centered between the two prongs. You pull back on your slingshot, hold the wood steady, and send the rock sailing through the air toward the bird. Way off in the distance, the bird is knocked off the branch.

"Yes!" You run through the trees to try to find the bird before it gets away. Dave, guessing that you must have gotten something, follows you. The trees are getting taller. You are no longer in the brush. The sun is blocked above your head. When you finally find the bird, it is in a musty grove of trees flapping along

the ground with a wounded wing. You race over and finish it with a quick shot in the head. Dave applauds. The African boys have also followed. They crowd around, grinning at you and speaking in Kiswahili.

"They're impressed," Dave translates. "They thought all outsiders were wimps and terrible shots, like I was when I first came. But they taught me well, and now I'm an expert!" He shoots a rock at a knot in a nearby tree. It hits the knot, ricochets off the tree and hits him in the nose. The African kids roar with laughter.

"I meant to do that," says Dave to you and then translates it into Kiswahili, making the kids laugh harder. "Let's go somewhere else while they're still laughing."

Dave says good-bye, and you walk away, each of you holding onto one of the bird's wings. "So," Dave asks as you walk along, "where'd you learn to shoot like that?"

You are beginning to tell him when a large dog comes racing out of trees, tearing toward the bird. You've got to think quickly.

(If you lift up the bird's wing, go to page 66.)
(If you drop the bird, go to page 69.)

You raise the slingshot until it is in a line with the bird. Holding the leather patch around the rock, you pull back firmly until the rubber strips are taut, and loose the rock in the bird's direction. The shot soars high over the bird's head and far off into the woods. The bird gives a low grating call and then flies away. It attracts the attention of the African boys and Dave, who regard its flight with disappointment. Dave sighs. "That kind of bird is delicious, but, oh well, you can't hit one every time you try." He shakes his head. The African boys chatter in Kiswahili, pointing at you and laughing. You tell Dave that you might as well go find your rock, just for an excuse to get away. There is a small commotion after you have headed off into the woods, but you ignore it, thinking they're still making fun of you.

As you pass through the trees, you stop dead. A large mangy dog, foaming at the mouth, is wandering aimlessly around in the clearing ahead. He is tripping over roots, bumping into trees and obviously is not very sure of himself. He must be sick, and he's probably wild. You try to sneak away, but the dog sees you. He starts toward you with a slow swagger. You turn to run and hear a low snarl. Looking over your shoulder, you see him limping toward you. You begin to run.

Jumping over bushes and trees, you run away from the rasping breath and snarls. You don't know where you are, and the dog is still chasing you. He is clumsy but determined. As you tear through the brush, you begin to trip over sticks and roots. You try to think of a way to get away from him. You could climb a tree, but then he could trap you at the bottom of it. You might be able to outrun him and get home before he catches you. He seems sick and slow enough, but what if you get lost?

(If you run until you find a tree, go to page 24.)
(If you try to make it home, go to page 28.)

A slingshot is an interesting contraption. You've been watching Dave shoot, so you have the general idea. You know to hold the base of the Y in one hand, put a rock into the leather cradle, pull back and let go toward the object you want to shoot. Besides being a large target, this bird moves very little. What could be more ideal? You wish that it were closer, though. You know you'll have to pull pretty hard to get the rock that far. You pick up the slingshot by the handle and aim for the bird. You pull back hard and let go. Somehow, the rock manages to hit one of the prongs of the Y instead of shooting through the middle. You'll never know how you did it. The rock bounces off the prong and lands in a nearby clump of grass. The African kids roar with laughter, and Dave looks up from where he has been searching for his latest rock. Hey, it was your first time to shoot a slingshot, so what's the big deal? You missed. Following Dave's example, you walk over to the clump of grass to find the rock (though, in your opinion, you have plenty of them in your pocket).

The laughing stops abruptly. As you reach the clump of grass, a rabbit darts out and runs between your legs. *"Sungura! Sungura!"* screams Dave. The chase is on! All is forgotten, your mistake, Dave's lost rock, and the enormous bird sitting in the far-off tree. The rabbit is all that matters. You and everyone else plunge through the woods after it. Dave races around another way and cuts it off from the front. In that split second in which the rabbit is deciding which way to dart next, an African boy jerks out a slingshot and, with one amazing shot, the rabbit carcass is lying on the ground.

You and Dave leave the woods and join the kids in the "rabbit parade" down the red-dirt village main street. All the villagers seem delighted. Apparently, getting a rabbit isn't an everyday occurrence. At the end of the street, the boy who shot the rabbit turns off into his yard. A delighted woman meets him. Dave greets her with *"Shikamo."*

She answers *"Marahaba"* and then faces the boy. She seems to be congratulating him. The boy begins speaking to her very quickly.

"What is he saying?" you ask Dave.

"I don't know," he replies. "I only speak Kiswahili, and he's speaking something else." Then the boy turns and says something to Dave. Dave smiles. "He would like to give us a back leg of the rabbit for our help in finding the rabbit and chasing it down. I'll tell him I accept it."

He replies to the boy in Kiswahili. The boy grins broadly. The woman takes the rabbit into the house and comes back with a small plastic bag with something long, lightweight and dirty-looking on the inside. Dave takes the bag and looks into it. He turns slightly green, then smilingly says thank you and good-bye before walking back down the street.

You and Dave have left the village and are heading down a gray, soft and sandy path through the brush that Dave *says* will lead to their family's driveway. The sand gives at every push of your feet, and walking down this path is wearing out your ankles. You just hope that it won't be too long now. The sun has gone behind a cloud, so at least you don't have to worry about *that* discomfort on this shadeless walk. "I'm really glad they gave us a bag," says Dave. "If we had walked back into the yard carrying a rabbit leg, Danielle would freak out. She's softhearted when it comes to animals. Once it's cooked up in a pot of soup, it's just meat, and she's fine." He looks into the bag and turns green again. "You know," he says, the normal color returning to his face, "if we had waited a little while longer, we could have gotten a *skinned* rabbit leg."

You hear the echo of a dog barking farther out in the brush, somewhere off to the right of the path. Dave is listening hard. "That sounds like our dog Simba. If it is, she's barking pretty frantically. It could be a wild dog, though. Should we go find out?"

(If you go to find out if it is Simba, go to page 42.)
(If you would rather go home and not risk a wild dog, go to page 55.)

You run with all your might. There has to be a tree big enough somewhere around here. For a sick animal floundering through bushes, that dog can certainly run! Finally, up ahead! You sprint and leap for the lowest branch, then scramble up faster than you ever knew you could, showering bark fragments and lichen all over the animal below. The dog stays snarling and slobbering at the bottom, but he can't get you. You're safe now, but your prediction was correct. The dog has trapped you in the tree. You try breaking off branches and throwing them at the dog, but it won't leave. You think of yelling for Dave but think better of it. If he comes here, he will have a wild dog to tangle with on the ground. You could yell to him and tell him *not* to come over here, but that's risky; he'd have to get close enough to understand you without attracting the attention of the sick animal.

You can't just sit here doing nothing, though; Dave's bound to start looking for you at some point.

As you sit there thinking about what to do next, a larger dog bursts through the brush. It snarls once at the dog under the tree. The mangy dog rises, growls and then runs in for the attack. In a flash, the larger dog flips the mangy one over on its back with a bite under its throat. The mangy dog manages to scratch the other dog's face, but no more. As soon as the bigger dog lets go, the other dog limps out of the clearing, its tail between its legs. The victorious dog barks threateningly at the clearing's edge, scaring the sick one farther away.

Danielle cautiously enters the clearing from the other side, looking around carefully.

"Danny!" you call and begin to climb out of the tree.

"Oh, there you are!" she says, shading her eyes and looking up. "Don't tell me, that wild dog I just saw chased you up there. Where's Dave?"

"He's over there somewhere." You point in the direction from which you came. The big dog, satisfied that the enemy has been scared away completely, comes trotting over as you reach the ground.

"I'm afraid of wild dogs," Danielle says. "That's why I brought Simba." At the sound of her name, Simba wags her tail and licks Danielle's hand. "That dog had rabies; I'm sure of it," Danielle says, looking at a patch of foaming slobber still at the base of the tree. Simba sniffs at it. Danielle grabs her collar and pulls her away. "Don't touch that, Simba! You've had your rabies shots, but that's still disgusting. We've got to go home and get Dad!"

"What's going on?" Dave emerges from the trees.

Danielle answers. "It just so happens that our guest was chased up a tree by a rabid dog. And where were you?"

"I was…well…somewhere else. Anyway," he turns to you, "you were smart to climb a tree, but Danielle's right, we've got to go home immediately to get Dad and the gun. Actually," he reconsiders, "you two go home and tell Dad. I'm going to take Simba and go back to warn those kids."

After you reach home and tell your story, Uncle Darryl takes his gun into the woods, along with a shovel. Two resounding shots tell you that you probably won't have to worry about that dog any more. "He's going to bury the carcass now," Danielle says, looking out a window at the back yard. "I'm so glad you didn't get bitten."

"And I'm glad that you brought the dog," you tell her. Danielle looks smugly at Dave and then turns away. When Dave returns from his errand of warning the African kids about the dog, he gives you an account of what happened. He didn't know the

Kiswahili word for rabies, so he had to act out the behavior of a rabid dog. The kids thought that it was pretty funny until they figured out what he was trying to say.

"Since there's rabies in the brush, maybe we should plan a canoeing trip for tomorrow," Danielle suggests.

"Yeah!" Dave agrees. "Just think, those islands out there are an untouched wilderness! No rabid dogs, no…."

"But there are pigs," Danielle reminds him. "Then again, it doesn't matter, since we won't actually be getting *off* on the islands."

Dave shuffles his feet and then winks at you. It's clear that tomorrow could be a very interesting day.

THE END

You run and run, but you must be lost. You are getting tired. The dog is drooling like mad but hasn't slowed a bit. You jump for a tree, but it's too late. The dog sinks its teeth into your leg. Your scream brings a large furry creature bounding out of the woods. It runs right up to the mangy dog and sinks its teeth into the back of its neck. The slobbering dog lets go of you to fight its attacker, but it is pushed down in a moment by the other dog. It gives up, whines and runs off as soon the larger dog loosens its grip. Your rescuer chases the dog a few feet and barks threateningly after it, as if to say, "And don't come back!" Danielle comes into view.

"Danny!"

"I was worried about the wild dogs and you guys out here, so I brought Simba. That dog looked rabid!"

Then she sees the teeth marks on your leg. "Oh, my goodness! Simba's had her rabies vaccinations, so she'll be okay, but you'll have to go to the city to get rabies shots. We've got to go home right now!" You can hear Dave calling your name. "Over here!" Danielle yells. Dave comes into view through the trees.

"What's going on?" he asks, seeing you sitting on the ground leaning up against a tree with Danielle standing over you looking terribly frightened. Danielle answers Dave's question quickly. "Our guest was bit by rabid dog, and we have to get out of the brush right now."

"Wait a minute. How do you know that the dog was rabid?" Dave asks.

"See that?" Danielle says furiously, pointing at the foamy slobbery mucus still left on your calf by the bite marks. "I saw the dog; I know it was rabid. It was alone, foaming at the mouth, attacked a person without provocation…." she sputters.

"Okay, I believe you!" Dave interrupts. He's staring at the bite on your leg and is also beginning to look a little scared. "You're right. We've got to get home, now! Can you walk?" he says to you. You nod and rise painfully.

You can tell on the way home that Danielle and Dave are trying to speed up the pace, but every step sends a burning pain through your calf muscles. The three of you reach the missionaries' driveway. As soon as you do, Dave runs on ahead of you into the house to tell his parents.

Aunt Debbie meets you inside the house with a basin of soap and water. You remember that she is a trained nurse and feel more confident that you'll be all right. After washing the wounds, she begins to apply Betadine, a red-brown cleansing agent. As she cleans your stinging wounds, she asks what happened. When you describe the behavior of the dog, she nods her head grimly. Aunt Debbie tells Dave and Danielle to pack seven outfits while Uncle Darryl radios for a plane. "From the way you've described the dog that bit you, I am very certain that it had rabies," Aunt Debbie tells you. "Solitude, swaggering and attacks are definitely symptoms of rabies. Even if we weren't sure about whether or not a dog that bit you had rabies, we would still take you into Mwanza to get you rabies shots. Rabies is not something to take chances on."

Uncle Darryl comes into the room and looks at your calf with its puncture wounds. "Ouch. Where was Simba when that dog attacked you?"

"Simba arrived after the dog had already bitten me; she scared it off," you tell him.

"David and Danielle!" Uncle Darryl calls. "Come out here, please." They come. "The next time anyone goes out in the brush, I want Simba to be with him or her from beginning to end. Do you understand?" They nod and go back to their rooms to finish packing. Aunt Debbie decides to fill you in on the treatment that you will receive.

"You're going to get eight shots," she informs you. "They will be spread out over about a month. It is the only treatment available here, but it is effective. Generally, when running from a dog, climbing a tree should be your immediate response. I'm not blaming this on you. If you had gone for a tree right away and hadn't gotten up it quickly enough, the dog could still have bitten you. Also, Simba should have been taken along from the start, but there's nothing we can do about that now. I'm sorry that this had to happen, but I'm sure that God has a good purpose for it. We will all fly out to the city with you tomorrow, and at least three of us will be with you the entire month. Uncle Darryl may come back early; we'll see."

Danielle comes in. "Dave and Simba have taken Dad out to where we last saw the dog. Dad is going to shoot and bury it. I didn't want to go; I've seen enough animals murdered in my lifetime." The sound of three gunshots out in the woods announce the end of the diseased animal.

That night at the regular 8:00 two-way radio call Uncle Darryl is able to charter a plane to arrive first thing in the morning to take you to Mwanza. You have to get your first shot within 24 hours after being bitten. That means before 2:30 p.m. tomorrow.

While you listen to the radio call, you are surprised to hear a man singing. Danielle explains. "That's the Mzinza padre who first introduced my family to the Wazinza. He commands a lot of respect in this area, and he liked the idea that we had come to be translators. So did the other Wazinza once he had introduced us. As you can hear," she smiles, "he also likes to sing. He's singing a spiritual song to encourage us."

The next morning you fly out in a little six-seater plane with the family and one pilot. After a half-hour flight to the Mwanza airport and an hour drive and wait at the clinic, you receive your first rabies shot. Your village adventure is over, but your African adventure isn't. Mwanza is a very interesting place.

THE END

"He said it wasn't very far," says Dave as he ducks under a vine, "but that's what they *always* say."

You and about 20 African kids are heading deeper into the woods. The trees are getting bigger. A canopy of branches blocks out most of the sunlight above your heads. You arrive in a clearing by a tree that must be at least 50 feet tall. Thirty feet up in the tangle of branches is a rusty old bicycle rim. It has no spokes and is stuck right-side-up in the branches.

"Kids around here roll old bicycle rims around for fun. They try to keep them moving and upright using only a straight stick. It's harder than it looks," Dave tells you, squinting up at the tire rim.

"So what's it doing up there?"

"They told me that about a year ago some kid named Kulua was mad at his brother Doto, so he threw Doto's tire rim up in the tree. No one was able to get it down, so they use it for target practice."

One by one the kids aim their slingshots at the rim. Some kids miss the tree entirely, but most kids lose their shots in the many branches and twigs. Finally the kid who challenged Dave drops his wild bird on the ground and steps toward the rim. The kids watch him respectfully as he carefully aims. The rock zips out of his slingshot. It soars up 35 feet, dodging perfectly between branches and then arches through the rim. The boys cheer. Then they all look at Dave.

Dave begins to sweat. With a slippery hand, he digs around in the rocks in his pocket. He pulls them all out and then carefully selects all the round ones. He then weighs each one individually on his palm. The dead silence under the tree is broken only by an occasional birdcall. All eyes are on Dave. He takes the chosen rock and turns it over and over, choosing the perfect side. He fits it into the pocket of the sling three times to make sure that it's right. He tugs on the rubber to be sure of its stability and pulls it back. Dave raises the slingshot, aims to the millimeter and lets the rock go. As if in slow motion the rock journeys upward. The tiny swish of the wind is all that can be heard. It goes up, then arches forward then slips through the center of the hoop. The exact center!

The clearing erupts in cheers! As the boys crowd around Dave giving him exuberant thumps on the back, his challenger walks over to shake his hand. Then Dave heads off to find his rock.

One boy walks over to you, points to your sling-shot, and then at the tire rim. Dave returns with his rock safely back in his possession. Now all eyes are on you.

(If you want to try shooting at the rim, go to page 39.)
(If you would rather not, go to page 51.)

"What was he yelling when we walked away from him?"

"Oh, he was calling us names because we wouldn't accept his 'challenge.' For all we know, he was going to tie a banana to your head and make me try to shoot at it. I get called names a lot, so it's no big deal."

"Like the way kids yelled, '*Wazungu!*' at the airport in Nairobi, Kenya?" you say, remembering what you heard shouted when you were there with Dave and Danielle.

"Yeah, only here in Kahunda we're called '*Bazungu.*' Both words refer to white people. Anytime a person with white skin comes into view, kids have to announce it, almost like you would in your country if a unicorn appeared. Some little African kids are terrified of white people. Their parents tell them that if they aren't good, the white people will come and get them. When I come into view, they run away screaming. I don't really blame them. Danielle has darker eyes, skin and hair, so she looks more like them. I guess she's not as scary as I am." Dave kicks a tuft of grass.

"So where are we going now?"

"Well, as long as we're hunting I thought that we might be able to go into the area of the brush with all the rabbit burrows. We could use a dog to scare them out, but maybe we'll be lucky without one."

You and Dave arrive at the first thicket. It is a bush overgrown inside and out with tall grass. "The rabbits dig their burrows under these thickets," Dave tells you. Just then a dog comes crashing out of the woods, knocks Dave down and starts barking joyously, slobbering all over his face.

"Simba! Just when I was thinking how much we needed a good dog on this trip, you come running out. Only a dog with a good sense of smell can figure out which rabbit burrows are inhabited."

"I thought you might need a dog," says Danielle, emerging from the trees behind you.

"So *you* brought her," says Dave looking disappointed. "All right, Danny, you can hunt with us, but don't talk this time. Last time I took you hunting you talked the whole way, and we didn't get anything."

"You never get rabbits when you go by yourself either," Danielle replies.

"Okay, you're right, I don't." He looks sheepishly at you. "But if you don't stop talking, you'll scare them all underground and we'll never get them out!" he finishes in a harsh whisper.

Simba has already begun running around sniffing the ground.

"My guess is that the commotion that Simba caused when she found you probably scared them all underground already," Danielle reasons out loud. "We should go somewhere else and then come back here more quietly."

"You're probably right," Dave agrees. "Besides, I'm thirsty. Let's go home and get something to drink."

"We could visit the pastor's house and ask them for a drink of water," Danielle suggests. "They boil their water, so we won't get sick. Besides, their house is closer than ours is."

"Sounds like a good idea," Dave replies. "Or we could just keep on hunting for a while somewhere else. My thirst can wait."

(If you want to go get a drink at the pastor's house, go to page 45.)
(If you want to just keep hunting, go to page 47.)

"So you are going to try it," says Dave matter-of-factly. "I'll warn you right now, it's really hard. Takes an expert shooter to...."

"Just be quiet, please?" You are trying to concentrate.

"Here," Dave says, "I'll even lend you my trusty rock. It's never failed me once."

"Oh, yeah, how many times have you used it?"

"Once."

Dave hands it to you. You look toward the hoop far above your head. Then you fit the rock into the slingshot. You carefully aim and then shoot. The rock is going too high! It arches then begins to go down. You hear the resounding ring as the rock hits the top of the hoop with full force, then the cracking of branches. The bicycle rim begins to fall. It lands with a thud on the forest floor. Dave's challenger runs up and grabs the hoop. As he sits there, holding it lovingly, Dave asks him a few questions. He comes back to you.

"That was his tire rim. He's Doto! Kulua and Doto are names the Luo fishermen give to any twin sons. He said that when his father's bicycle wore out, his father gave a wheel rim to each of his sons. Kulua took his wheel rim with him when they went out fishing and lost it over the side of the boat. He thought that, being the older twin, he should get Doto's wheel rim, but his father didn't agree. His father told Kulua that if he was careless enough to take his toys out on fishing trips and lose them, he didn't deserve another wheel rim. Doto made fun of him, so Kulua took Doto's wheel rim into the woods and threw it up in that tree.

"Doto discovered that once the wheel was stuck up in a tree it was only good for target practice. Now you have gotten his wheel rim back."

The other boys have begun to leave the clearing. Doto thanks you for retrieving his wheel, picks up his dead bird and then leaves. Dave sighs. "Now that that wheel is gone, how in the world am I going to find anything challenging to shoot at?" You point to a bird roosting in a nearby tree. It is small but fat. Dave whips out his slingshot and shoots. The rock misses the bird, scaring it away. Dave sends a few frantic looks around him, then seeing that you were the only one who saw that, sighs with relief. "Let's get going."

"What about your trusty rock?"

"Oh, yeah, I'll let you in on a secret. It wasn't really the rock that was responsible for my," he clears his throat, "exceptionally accurate and well-aimed bull's-eye, it was…."

"Yeah, yeah."

You and Dave wander around for a while in the brush and sun and then decide to head home. You didn't get any game, but you did get the reputation of being excellent shooters and, of course, a new friend.

THE END

You follow the barking through the under-growth. As you arrive in a small clearing, you see a strange sight. At one end of the clearing a small chicken is pecking at bugs on the ground. At the other end Danielle is grasping a tree with one hand and Simba's collar with the other. The dog is straining toward the chicken. Danielle looks like she'll be ripped apart. Dave drops the bag and grabs Simba's collar. He holds on as she barks, jumps and strains to get at the chicken. Danielle collapses in a relieved heap.

"So what's going on? No, don't tell me," says Dave, holding back the lunging dog. "I think I can fig-ure it out."

Danielle strides across the clearing, grabs the chicken and holds it upside-down by its feet. It

squawks for a minute and then hangs still and sub-
dued with its wings out.

"I sent Simba out here to locate you because I
was bored, and I thought that you might like to have a
dog with you on your hunting trip."

"A good assumption," says Dave.

"Well, I commanded Simba to find you, and she
found Fryer Cluck."

"You told Simba to find me, and she found your
pet chicken?" asks Dave with a puzzled expression on
his face. "What description of me did you give her?"

"Ha, ha," says Danielle. "Well, I'm glad you came
around when you did. What's in the bag?"

"You probably don't want to know." Dave swats
the dog over the head a few times and lets her go. Too
late he remembers that he dropped the bag on the
ground. Simba trots right across the clearing and
picks it up. She begins to walk away as if to find a nice
comfortable patch of grass where she can gnaw her
lucky find in peace. Dave lunges for the bag. She
begins to run. He misses the bag with the rabbit leg in
it but manages to grab hold of Simba's heavy tail. She
yelps. He crawls forward, grabs the bag out of her
mouth and begins a tug-of-war. Within a minute the
bag is so mangled and bloody that he gives it up and
allows Simba to go off with her hard-earned prey.

"What was in there?" Danielle asks, looking disgustedly at the bloody slobber and slime all over Dave's hands.

"Our hunted quarry," Dave replies, "or part of it, anyway."

You all head for home.

Aunt Debbie greets you at the back door. "How was your hunting trip? Oh, I see you brought home a *chicken?*"

Danielle sighs. "No way, Mom. We're not eating Fryer Cluck, and Simba already got whatever Dave brought back."

"Oh, well," Aunt Debbie sighs.

THE END

The four of you walk out of the woods and stand at the bottom of a hill. You can see the pastor's house at the top. It isn't a typical African house. Missionaries built this house many years ago. Simba is excited.

"You know," says Danielle warily, "I don't think that we should take Simba with us. The pastor's family has a lot of chickens, and, well, you know how Simba is."

"Yeah," Dave agrees. "I'll hold on to the dog, and you two go up the hill first to ask for a drink of water."

"But you're the one who's thirsty!" Danielle exclaims.

"I know," Dave says. "But you're the one who can speak Kiswahili well. By the time I'm done trying to explain that I'd like some water and could you save some for my sister because she's down holding the dog while I get water so that our dog won't kill the chickens and that I'm going down to take her place, etc., it will be time to go home. You go up and explain it, and then when I go up there, I won't have to talk at all. They'll hand me the water and I'll say '*asante*' and be done with it."

"Okay," says Danielle. "Then again," she turns on you, "*you* could stay and hold the dog. Then *I'll* go up and do all the talking, and Dave can get his water. Unless, of course, you're thirsty too."

(If you'll wait and hold onto Simba, go to page 131.)
(If you'd rather walk and get a drink of water with Danielle, go to page 136.)

Dave crawls off through the thickening brush, followed by Simba.

You and Danielle creep along after him. "I think he's heading for the airstrip," Danielle predicts. You look up. Ahead through the scrub trees you glimpse a wide green field, with the blue of Lake Victoria beyond. As you duck under a bush, you see Dave standing on the other side, holding a handful of small rocks. He's throwing the rocks some 18 feet up into the air. Your eyes locate his target just in time to see a fish fall from the talons of an eagle screeching overhead. Danielle dashes over to a clump of tall grass, reaches in a hand and picks up the fish gasping out its last breath. It flips quickly. "Ouch," says Danielle and drops it.

"You remember, sharp fins?" says Dave, walking over to her. "At the moment," says Danielle, clutching her hand as blood slowly seeps out from between her other fingers, "how could I possibly forget? Ouch."

Dave considers her hand as she gingerly takes her other hand off it. You walk over too. The skin between her thumb and forefinger is deeply cut. "You'll have to get stitches on that," Dave says with certainty. "Noooo," says Danielle, clutching her hand again. "I don't want stitches."

"You'll have to get them if your hand is going to heal right."

"Or 'heal properly,' as Mom would say."

Dave turns his attention to the clump of grass. "What a beauty!" he says as he carefully picks up the fish by the gills.

"It is," Danielle agrees, without a lot of heart in her voice.

Dave looks back over at Danielle's hand. "I think that we'd better start heading home."

"So," says Dave, happily swinging the fish in his hand, "our hunting trip was successful after all!" He looks down at the fish and then starts, as though seeing it for the first time. His mood darkens and he gets a worried look on his face. Danielle looks upset too.

"I'm not sure if we should have taken the fish from the fish eagle. It's not nice."

"If you're worried about the fish eagle," Dave replies, "it can always get another fish without a lot of difficulty." Dave still looks worried.

"What's the matter, Dave?" Danielle asks.

Dave scrutinizes the fish again. "I think this fish is bloated. No, I'm *sure* it is."

Danielle stops dead in her tracks and comes back to look at the fish. "Poisoned fish are bigger around! That one's just fat."

"Poisoned?" you ask.

"The fishermen around here sometimes poison the water. Many fish in the area die, bloat up and then float to the surface, where they are easily harvested. However, it isn't safe to eat a poisoned fish," Dave explains.

"I don't think it's been poisoned," Danielle stubbornly insists. "We'll take it back, and if Mom and Dad say we can't eat it, we won't. Otherwise I don't see a problem."

"The problem is that we can't know for sure. We should get rid of it somewhere where no one can find it. How about if we bury it?"

"Simba will dig it up! I say we take it home."

"Mom and Dad won't know for sure if it's poisoned either," Dave continues insistently. "Besides, it's *my* fish; I *got* it from the fish eagle! If it's poisonous, *I* should be the one to dispose of it."

"It's probably fine!" Danielle turns to you. "What do you think that we should do?"

(If you decide that the fish is safe and edible, go to page 71.)
(If you don't want to risk eating the fish, go to page 73.)

Jeers and jibes follow you as you and Dave leave the clearing. "It's the same in any country," Dave tells you. "You pass up a challenge and you get made fun of. It isn't such a big deal for you, though; you're leaving in a few weeks. If I had passed up that shooting challenge, I would never have lived it down. So why didn't you try it?" You don't have time to answer his question; he keeps on talking. "Wasn't I great? I can't believe that I made that shot! I not only made the shot, I made the bull's-eye!"

You and Dave leave the tall, tangled trees of the woods and reenter the gnarly growth of the brush. After walking for a while, you cross a sandy road. It's called "the new road" and leads to the airstrip and the ferry landing. You reenter the brush on the other side of the road and head down a narrow, sandy path.

"Well, whatdya know?" Dave says comically as you enter a clearing in the brush. A large gunnysack, obviously full, is hanging from a gnarly brush tree. A pile of ashes nearby also serves to prove the presence of man. "We are in luck!" Dave walks over to the gunnysack and begins sizing it up from all angles. He winds up and flings a hard punch at the sack. He staggers back gasping and holding his fist. "It got me!" Dave falls listless on the sand. He soon offers an explanation for his confusing behavior. "We seem to have stumbled across the secondary school's punching bag! The secondary school is kind of like a high school only with older students in something that they call 'forms' instead of grades. The school is about a 10- to 15-minute walk from here. Danielle probably wouldn't like this place, though. She wouldn't want to meet up with any of the students. They're all male and they like to 'tease,' or rather, pick on her. She hates it."

Dave is still lying on the ground when Simba arrives. Danielle comes into the clearing while Simba is busy trying to slobber all over his face. "The secondary school punching bag!" she says with surprise. She winds up a careful punch. "Ouch. This thing doesn't give at all! It's like hitting a rock."

"I know," says Dave, rubbing his bruised knuckles. "It's supposed to teach you how to perfect your punches, so that if you really did have to punch something bulky and hard you could do so without injury." He looks down at his fist. "My hand obviously wasn't positioned properly."

Male voices are approaching through the brush.

"Dave, let's go, please?" Danielle pleads.

"Yeah, if you stay here, and those are the secondary students, I may really have to punch someone. Let's go." The three of you leave the clearing with Danielle and Simba in the lead. You might never know who was really coming, but it wasn't worth waiting around to find out.

You are at the back of the line, with Dave, Danielle and Simba in front. As you walk past a leafy scrub tree, out of the corner of your eye you notice that there is a large black hole going under the roots. Out of curiosity, you turn around to look back. The hole is about a foot to a foot and a half wide and goes back farther than you can see. You'd like to go back and look down the hole, or burrow probably, but you wonder if that would be a good idea. A moment later you *know* that it wouldn't have been a good idea. A large, crocodile-like reptile is crawling out of the hole. It crawls quickly and purposefully. It's at least six feet long from head to tail. It stops to look at you. The others have gone on ahead.

(If you call for Simba, go to page 142.)
(If you stand still, go to page 145.)
(If you run away after the others, go to page 149.)

"When we get home, we can see if Simba's there," says Dave. "Even if that is our dog, she's probably just barking at monkeys." You push your way out of the brushy woods and into Dave's yard. Aunt Debbie meets you at the back door. "So, you guys actually got something? That's great. What is it?"

"Well, actually we found it and one of the African boys killed it."

"What is it?" Aunt Debbie asks again.

"A rabbit leg," says Dave.

"Well, put it in the freezer right away; I've already got dinner planned for tonight."

"Ah, Mom! You knew we were going hunting!"

His mom raises her eyebrows.

"Okay, so I don't usually get anything."

There is a rustling in the woods at the back of the yard. You see Danielle come out of the woods, holding something in her arms. Simba is trotting along beside her, looking confused and consoling as Danielle sobs and angrily holds the object out of the dog's reach. *"Nita kuchapa!"*

"A wounded animal," Dave surmises. "Danny hates monkeys, so it wouldn't be one of those."

"Besides," says Aunt Debbie, "Danielle knows better than to hold a monkey or any strange animal, for that matter. A monkey could have AIDS or rabies or—oh, no!"

"What?" you ask.

"It's Fryer Cluck," Aunt Debbie says as she rushes off the porch toward Danielle.

"Fryer Cluck is Danny's pet chicken," Dave explains. "Our night-time security guard gave it to her. We used to tease her about having a pet *chicken*, but any teasing from us about eating her pet would leave her crying, so we stopped. She has gotten very attached to the poor thing. It earns its keep, lays an egg about every other day. It's just hard to take care of and keep safe. What with dogs, chicken hawks, genet cats and mongooses, how are we supposed to keep that bird alive?"

You and Dave follow Danielle inside. The chicken's breathing is labored, and it is wounded at the neck. Danielle gets it a bowl of food and some water. She sets the chicken comfortably down on an old towel on the workroom floor. "Normally we would never allow a chicken in the house," Dave tells you. "But this is an exception."

Danielle is sitting, staring dully at the chicken. Aunt Debbie draws you aside. "This may seem like a lot of fuss to be made over a pet, especially a pet chicken," Aunt Debbie explains. "But Danielle is very lonely. Did you see any kids out in the woods today?"

"Yes," you answer.

"Any girls?"

"No."

"Girls in this culture have to work at home," Aunt Debbie continues. "Danielle has her brother and the African boys to hang around with, but female friends are harder to come by. Danielle gets lonely. Lonely people tend to be more attached to their pets. I'm sure she's glad that you could be with us for a while."

You are beginning to understand a little more about life for this missionary family. For the time being, you'll wait and see what happens. Aunt Debbie says that chickens are supposed to be quick healers. For Danielle's sake, you hope so.

THE END

You and Dave duck to avoid the hanging vines and thorn bushes. "We're almost there!" Dave calls. With all the small damp dead leaves stuck to your knees, you're glad. "One last vine," Dave steps over a vine about two inches in diameter covered with bark and half-inch thorns, "and we're here!" You are no longer in "the brush," as David and Danielle call it. You are now in "the jungle." The jungle resembles a real jungle with vines hanging everywhere and trees that cut out most of the light. The brush had almost no real shade at all. Now you are surrounded by it. You are standing in between 4 or 5 trees, all about 30 feet tall with smooth bark and many twisting branches. No tree in this jungle grows higher than 50 feet. Perfect for climbing.

"Now," Dave is explaining, "normally, safety rules are as follows. If attacked by a wild animal, like a

wild dog, you should climb a tree. If there are no trees, you should jump into the lake. If the lake is too far away, you grab a stick. In all of the above cases, you yell for help. Here in the jungle, however, the animals are different.

"If you see a snake, it is a good idea to cautiously escape on the ground. Snakes normally would rather run away from you than attack. If you see a monkey, don't act scared, pick up a stick, and walk away. If you are in a tree, get out of it! Monkeys are dangerous. They can sit up to four feet tall, and they have killer teeth. They also spread rabies and AIDS. If you see a monkey without a tail—in other words, a baboon—go home as fast as you can. We don't get them here very often, but when one is sighted, everyone stays out of the brush and the jungle for weeks. They are much stronger than humans are and, as the Africans say, 'If you throw a spear at a baboon, he will catch it and throw it back.' Besides, a baboon is likely to have better aim than you do.

"Which brings me back to the point," says Dave, suddenly cheerful again. "Danny and I have an escape plan all worked out from this tree! Observe the Monkey-Escape." Dave starts climbing a tree nearby and you follow him up. All you see are two branches about three inches in diameter, sticking straight out from the large one that you and Dave are sitting on. "Normally this would be a 10- or 11-foot drop." Dave sits on the lower branch, grabs the other one about two feet in front of him and drops off the one that he is sitting on. He swings from his hands and then drops, feet first, to the ground. "Bend your knees when you hit the ground. If you're too stiff, you could break a bone, and then I would get in trouble." Dave begins climbing up the tree again. "Danny and I cleared all the brush out from under the monkey-escape, so you don't need to worry about landing on anything. Well, go ahead! This is practice. And besides, it's kind of fun."

There is a crashing of foliage off in the distance behind you. "Could be monkeys coming this way; I guess you won't have time for practice. As soon as you see a monkey, jump for it. I'll be right behind you." A stout animal bursts into the clearing and races under the branch you were just about to jump from. A large dog is in pursuit. "Oh, yes, I forgot," Dave wipes his brow. "When you see a badger, it is best to stay in your tree. Badgers generally live underground, but they can put up a good fight." He looks back in the direction the dog appeared from. "Danny?"

"Yes?"

"What are you doing here?"

Danielle begins climbing up the tree.

"I sent Simba to find you guys, and she just took off a little ways back. I had all I could do to keep up with her."

"I can see that," says Dave as Danielle begins climbing the tree. When she reaches him, he pulls a thorn branch out of her hair. She begins pulling sharp stickers off her long skirt.

"Climbing trees in a long skirt is quite an art!" she laughs. "It can be done. I still think that life would be more fun if I didn't have to wear one. In African culture, girls are expected to wear skirts."

"Danny, you're planting sticker bushes all over the landing for the monkey-escape!" Dave looks down at the carefully cleared area where all the seeds are falling. Danielle begins to throw her seeds off to the side.

"We have never really had to use this thing anyway."

"We might, though. There are a lot of monkeys around here," Dave counters.

"You guys certainly found the thorn bushes," says Danielle, eyeing the tiny scratch marks on you and Dave. She sees one rather large scratch on Dave's back. "That one looks pretty serious!"

"That was the compliments of a mother bird who obviously didn't want her little bird returned to her nest."

The sound of a frantically barking dog is heard off in the distance.

"Maybe we should go check on Simba," Danielle suggests.

"Naw, I'd like to show our guest another tree. How about Goliath?" He grins wickedly.

"Simba might be in trouble!"

"Naw, she just sounds excited. Besides, if she's cornered the badger, we don't want to be around."

Danielle is determined. "We can do Goliath another day; you just want to put our guest on the Fr…."

"Shhhhh!" Dave interrupts her. "It has to be a surprise."

Danielle turns to you. "I guess it's up to you. What do you want to do?"

(If you want to go check on Simba, go to page 83.)
(If you would rather go to Goliath, go to page 84.)

As you walk through the brush, Dave suddenly dashes ahead of you. He jumps over a small bush up ahead and disappears from view. After doing a quick check for whatever made him dash off like that, you follow. You find yourself standing at the edge of a circular pit about 40 feet wide and 20 feet deep. Dave is nowhere in sight. You remember that he mentioned that there were *two* sandpits. "Hey! Over here!" You hear a voice from off in the brush to your right. You follow it and find yourself standing looking over a slightly smaller pit at Dave who seems to be balancing on thin air about five feet from the pit's edge. A closer examination reveals a tree root sticking out from the side of the pit on which Dave is precariously balancing. You watch as he begins doing graceful pirouettes on the bouncy root and then totters, wavers, falls and rolls down to the bottom. After brushing himself off, he sees you standing on the edge of the pit and insists that you try it.

You hear a large group of children's voices, getting nearer. "Sounds like a group of African boys coming to share the pits with us. We can stay and share it with them or go somewhere else."

(If you stay, go to page 76.)
(If you decide to leave before they arrive, go to page 80.)

You lift up the bird's wing. The dog, however, makes a valiant leap in the air, grabs the bird and tears off through the woods. "Oh, great!" Dave runs after the dog. Danielle appears from across the clearing, grasps the situation and joins in the chase. You run too; after all, it's your bird! Danielle has taken a different route. "Try to cut her off!" Dave yells back at you.

"Who?" you yell without thinking.

"Simba!" Dave screeches. "I'll keep chasing her toward the house; you try to get in front of her!"

Not sure exactly what to do, you run to the right. That is probably the direction of the house, since that is the way that you and Dave were heading home. This place is new to you, though, so you can't be sure. Seeing a clear area up ahead through the trees, you run for it. You are on a sandy road, probably the missionaries' driveway. Hearing a commotion in the woods, you look at a large pile of leaves in front of the trees by the driveway. The sound is definitely coming towards the leaves. Simba leaps over the pile of leaves, not knowing that you are standing in her path. You grab her collar and hold on tight. The momentum of Simba's jump pulls you to the ground, but you've caught her.

Danielle appears from nowhere and pulls the bird from the mouth of the surprised dog. "Well-done." Dave takes Simba's collar from you. You gladly stand up. Your shirt is full of sand from your being dragged across the sandy driveway. By the time you and Dave reach the house, Danielle has taken the bird safely inside.

"A few teeth marks," she comments, "but since we're going to cook it, it should be okay."

Aunt Debbie has other concerns. "Is this bird a fish-eating bird? You're never supposed to eat those."

"I don't think so," says Danielle. "The Africans eat this bird, and I've always seen them on land, never in the lake water. I can't believe you guys got something this big!"

"Well," Dave coughs, "actually, our guest is responsible for this bird." Danielle is impressed. That afternoon is spent cleaning and preparing the bird. You and the family roast it that evening in a little

African charcoal oven called a *jiko*. The bird doesn't have a whole lot of meat on it, but it's pretty good with salt.

THE END

You drop the bird, but Dave has another idea. As soon as you have let go, he whips the bird over to his side and out of the way of the dog. "No, Simba! Down!"

"Come, Simba!" The commanding tone used by Danielle across the clearing is enough to stop Simba's jumping, for a moment. Danielle crosses the clearing, takes hold of Simba's collar and holds it firmly.

"So you finally showed up, Danny." Dave starts heading home. "I thought that you didn't want to hunt." Simba follows, dragging Danielle, her eyes on the large bird.

"So you guys actually got something? Already?" Danielle sounds impressed.

"Yup. You didn't know that our guest was good with a slingshot, did you?"

"Well, no, I didn't." Simba gives a hard jerk on Danielle's hand, still holding on to her collar. Danielle opens her mouth to scold the dog.

"Wait a minute!" Dave peers through the trees at the yard up ahead. "It looks like we've got company!"

Through the trees you catch a glimpse of a herd of goats that must have wandered into the missionaries' yard, munching happily.

"They'll eat the tomato vines!" Danielle exclaims indignantly. "Sic 'em, Simba!" Simba peers up at her doubtfully, surprised that she is actually being *asked* to chase goats. "Go on!" Danielle urges her.

Simba races into the yard, barking joyously and scattering goats right and left. Eventually they're all chased out. You prepare the bird and roast it over a little African charcoal oven called a *jiko* that evening. Simba and the cat get the leftovers, though there aren't very many; just bones to be cleaned.

The End

"I think we can probably eat the fish," you decide. "After all, if the fishermen had poisoned the water recently, wouldn't there be other fish floating around on top of the water?"

"Unless the fisherman already harvested them all," Dave argues. Danielle agrees with your logic, however, and the three of you take the fish home. You receive an "okay" from their mom and dad to eat the fish. Both parents are surprised that the three of you brought home a fish from your hunting trip, but Danielle's story about how Dave knocked it from the talons of a fish eagle with a rock makes sense to them. Uncle Darryl guts the fish for you and Danielle while Danielle gets the cut on her hand numbed and stitched up by Aunt Debbie, a nurse. Dave refuses to eat any of it, so you and Danielle enjoy the fruits of your hunting trip that evening: fish roasted over a little African charcoal oven called a *jiko*.

All in all, it was a good day. Not only that, neither you nor Danielle get sick from the fish. You took a risk but made a correct decision.

THE END

"We shouldn't eat the fish," you decide. "One fish isn't worth the risk of getting poisoned." Danielle pouts slightly but seems convinced. When you reach the house, Danielle goes inside to get the cut in her hand cleaned, numbed and stitched up by her mother, a trained nurse. You and Dave toss the fish into the garbage pit, the hole in the ground in the back of the missionaries' yard where the family burns trash, hoping that it will be burned later with the next load of garbage. Simba, however, jumps into the pit and grabs the fish. Dave catches her on the way out and puts the fish up in a tree nearby where Simba can't get it, planning to put it back into the pit in the morning.

That evening you and the family sit around a little African charcoal oven called a *jiko* roasting marshmallows mailed to the family by a friend back in their home country. You hear a snarling sound nearby. Dave gets a flashlight and gasps. Their cat is sitting on the ground near the warmth of the fire, pulling and snarling at an already half-eaten fish. She blinks, her fluorescent eyes glowing yellow in the light of the flashlight, and then continues tearing at the carcass. "No!" Dave runs over and gingerly takes the fish from the growling cat. "It's for your own good, Chiro!" he explains. Chiro stops growling and tries a different tactic. She rubs around his legs and meows sweetly and hungrily, begging him to return her fish.

"She's not really hungry," Danielle observes, cradling her bandaged hand. "She's eaten more than half of it."

"If she's eaten that much, I guess that there's no hope for her." Dave drops the fish, and Chiro drags it off, snarling at it once again.

"There *might* be no hope; you're the one who said that we couldn't know for sure whether or not the fish was poisoned," Danielle reminds him.

"So how did the cat get the fish?" asks Uncle Darryl.

"I put it up in a tree so that Simba couldn't get it," Dave answers. "I didn't think of Chiro."

"We'll just wait and see what happens." Aunt Debbie stares off into the dark toward the direction of the delighted snarling of the feline gorging itself on its hard-earned prey. "At least she'll die happy."

"Mom!" Danielle doesn't agree with this logic.

The cat didn't die. It stayed healthy for several more years, a sure sign that the fish had not been poisoned after all. But better to be safe than sorry.

THE END

The babble of voices gets louder as the group of African kids approaches the sandpits. "Can you understand what they're saying?" you ask Dave.

"Nope, I only speak—well, half speak—the national language, Kiswahili. They're speaking another language; who knows which one?"

The kids, all boys as Dave predicted, have arrived at the first pit. They begin a game of king-of-the-mountain at the edge of the pit, or perhaps called king-of-the-ridge. The game consists of a wrestling match. It isn't over until only one person is standing at the top of the pit. The others, pushed off the edge and into the pit, are free to come back up and get pushed off again. Since the pit is composed of soft sand, being pushed into it looks like fun. Dave obviously thinks so. One kid is left alone at the top of the pit. He is one of the largest. "How old do you think he is?" you ask Dave.

"I know him. He's 14." The kid must be quite small for his age.

"What about the smallest one?" you ask.

"Who, him? About 6 or 7 years old, I would guess." At this rate, all of the kids must be small for their ages. Dave seems to know what you're thinking. "Kids here hit their growth spurts later."

Just then Simba comes leaping through the woods and jumps over a bush at the edge of the pit. Surprised at the sudden drop-off, she paws the air frantically before rolling down to the bottom. "The next arrival will be a girl," Dave predicts. Sure enough, the next to jump over the bush and roll down into the pit is Danielle. She laughs and dusts off her long skirt. "So, Danielle, you've finally found a way to combat the parachute effect."

"Dave, that's mean! Before he explains it," she turns to you, "I will. The parachute effect is what happened when I first tried jumping into the pit with a long full skirt. My skirt caught the air and ballooned out. Anyway, he was behind me, waiting to jump, so it's not like he saw anything. He has no idea how annoying it is to have to wear long skirts and dresses all the time!" She gets up and eyes your torn clothes strangely. "What happened, did you guys go through some thorn bushes? Your clothes are in shreds! And, Dave, you're bleeding!"

"How bad is it?" Dave asks, trying to see the cut on his back. It is impossible.

"Not too bad," Danielle reassures him.

The African boys at this point have stopped their game in the other pit and are coming over to yours, obviously happy to see the three of you.

Danielle recognizes some of them. "They used to be surprised to see me out here," she tells you. "Girls in their culture generally have a lot of house-work to do at home. Some boys have the job of herding animals, but most of them don't have to work much. That's why they have time to play. Now they've gotten used to seeing me with Dave, and I doubt they give my presence very much thought anymore."

Simba, meanwhile, has been floundering around in the brush beside the pit. She's picked up an interesting scent. The African boys have begun somersaulting, cartwheeling, and flipping down the steepest sandy slope. "You know, Dave, I don't think we've ever really explored the brush on the other side of the sandpits," Danielle remarks.

"I have," Dave says flatly. "That's where all the rabbit burrows are. I've explored it when I've gone rabbit hunting with friends. It isn't very exciting and you almost never get a rabbit."

"We don't have to hunt," Danielle persists. "We can just explore!"

"I told you, it's not very exciting!" Dave repeats. "Besides, I'm tired and I think that we should go home."

"What do you want to do?" Danielle gives you the job of resolving the issue.

"I'm going home, whatever you decide," Dave declares.

(If you go with Danielle to explore around the rabbit burrows, go to page 153.)
(If you return home with Dave, go to page 157.)

You and Dave disappear into the trees just as the hum of voices reaches the pits. "We could have stayed," Dave says slightly regretfully. "They usually play games like king-of-the-mountain on the edge of the pit. Then again, exploring some more could be fun too."

You and Dave leave the path and enter a brushy area. This quickly gives way to taller trees. The lighting is filtered, and dead leaves cover the ground. You and Dave are silent. The undergrowth starts getting thicker and taller. Eventually it's above your heads except for dog trails underneath. You and Dave find yourselves crawling. "I don't know if I've ever been here before." Dave frowns as he looks at the ground, only about a foot away from his face. "No worries; we can't get lost! These woods only extend about a mile on any side before you hit a dirt road or a path or...."

He doesn't finish. Dave is on his hands and knees beside you, staring transfixed at a wound pile of shiny black coils in front of him. Large ones. As you gaze, transfixed as well, the coil nearest to you begins to casually unwind. "Run!" shrieks Dave. He flips around and then crashes back in the direction that you came, clumsily bumbling on all fours but making surprising progress for a natural biped. You turn on your hands and knees and find yourself tangled in a bush. You quickly struggle free. As you prepare to follow Dave, a thought crosses your mind. Will you scramble off with all haste, or dare look back?

(If you follow Dave's example and crawl off immediately, go to page 87.)
(If you look back, go to page 89.)

"I think we should go see why Simba is barking," you say.

"Okay," Dave pushes past you and swings down out of the monkey-escape. You see that the escape has more than one good use. It is not only a way to escape danger, it is also an easy descent from the tree. Danielle follows Dave, swings out on the branch and drops. It's obvious that she's had practice too. They then wait on the ground for you to try it.

(If you try swinging down from the monkey-escape,
go to page 160.)
(If you would rather just climb down the tree, go to page 161.)

"Dave!" Danielle says in a muffled voice, as a leafy branch swings back in her face, "remember your trail etiquette and be considerate of the person behind you, especially if they are a head shorter than you are."

"Sorry." Dave is serious for a moment, and then his face goes right back to the weird grin he got when you said that you wanted to go see the tree that they call Goliath.

"Secondly, if *it* didn't scare you, why are you so eager to put all of our friends onto *it?*"

"Because *it* is a *challenge!*"

"Oh, all right, but I don't want you to dare our guest onto *it* like you did last time."

The three of you emerge from the jungle, cross a gray sandy road and then enter a jungle on the other side. This area is more light and airy than the part with the monkey-escape, probably because the trees here are taller. There are fewer thorn bushes and no thorn vines. "This is the tree of the famous 'winding staircase,'" Danielle informs you as you pass a tree with a large branch shaped like a corkscrew going up through the middle of it. "And here is the vine swing that we had to re-hang in the tree four times."

"Whenever I tried to swing on it," Dave informs you, "it broke. And here we are." You are looking at the largest tree that you have seen yet. A large tree of twisting smooth branches is rising up out of the forest floor. "And may I present," Dave pauses dramatically and then points straight above his head, "the challenge of the Freaky Seat!"

Thirty feet above you two thick branches have grown out over the forest floor. They entwine and bend down and then up, forming a bucket on which to sit, before their ends disappear into the canopy overhead. "Well?" Dave wants to know, "are you equal to the challenge?"

"We could always go to the Eagle's Nest," Danielle suggests, obviously trying to give you another option.

"What's the Eagle's Nest?" you ask.

"Well, as you can see, the branches of these trees form a canopy over the ground. The Eagle's Nest is a tree that we have found with a way to get up and sit on top of the canopy. The view is incredible. Of course," she says cautiously, looking at Dave, but talking to you, "we can always go there *after* you finish the challenge of the Freaky Seat."

(If you decide that you will accept the challenge of making it to and sitting in the Freaky Seat, go to page 90.)
(If you decide that you would rather go to the Eagle's Nest, go to page 113.)

You follow Dave's example and scurry off as quickly as you can. Following the trail of mussed leaves, you are able to get out. You hear Dave calling your name up ahead. You crawl out from under a thicket and stand up.

"What took you so long?"

"I got caught on a bush."

"Oh. I thought that maybe you had been bitten, or spit on, or perhaps hypnotized." Dave crosses his eyes and moves his head from side to side.

"What am I doing?" he comes out of his feigned hypnosis immediately. "We've got to get out of here! Watch your step, but hurry. They say that when you see a snake you're never supposed to run away because it might have a mate nearby, but that doesn't apply here in Tanzania, as I understand it. Snakes never travel in pairs, and it isn't worth waiting around when so many snakes are deadly." You and Dave hurry off. "The next time I go crawling through woods like that, I'll definitely have a dog with me," he says.

You have reached the family's sandy driveway. Dave keeps peering back nervously behind you. When you arrive home, their parents get out the family snake book. Only one snake fits your and Dave's description. This is the 1.2-meter, nocturnal, black-necked spitting cobra. You read that a spitting cobra can send well-aimed jets of damaging venom into the eyes of its prey or aggressor, blinding the opponent temporarily or permanently, but certainly long enough for the snake to get away. You did well not to look back.

THE END

You turn your head and stare straight into the eyes of a hooded cobra just in time to see two streams of liquid venom shoot toward your eyes.

(If you are wearing glasses right now [contacts don't count], go to page 98.)
(If you are not wearing glasses, go to page 129.)

Climbing Goliath takes a lot of balance and arm strength. Danielle is skillfully making her way up behind you in her culturally required long full skirt while Dave stands on the ground under the Freaky Seat just to let you know how high up you are. "I discovered the Freaky Seat a few years ago," Danielle tells you. "I wasn't wearing a long skirt that day; people around here don't care as much what anyone wears during their younger years. I was climbing up ahead of Dave and some boys when I saw it. Naturally it looked like the perfect place to sit. I crawled out over the two branches to it. When I finally reached it and sat down, I found out about the freaky nature of the seat. The tree was swaying in the wind. I had no back to lean against, nowhere to put my feet, and nothing to hold onto except what I was sitting on. There was nothing to break my fall before I hit the ground below. The ground itself was as far away as six people my height all standing on one another's shoulders; though, believe me, from up there it looks farther. The boys by this time had climbed to the edge of the two branches that I was sitting on. They couldn't go any further with me sitting out there, so they sat down to enjoy the scenery. I was petrified by then; my hands were cramping from holding on so hard. I pleaded with them to move so that I could get out but they wouldn't." She glares down at Dave. "After begging and pleading for a while, I finally told them that I was sitting in the most terrifying place in the world. They said that it didn't look that scary. I said that if they sat on it, they *would* be scared."

Danielle pauses the story while she instructs you on where to grab and where to step as you cross between 2 branches over a 20-foot drop. There aren't many places to put your feet, and it is important which foot you put first. "You will need your right foot free for the next step," Danielle reiterates, "so be sure that you step across with your left, even if it feels awkward. As I was saying," Danielle continues, "they insisted that the seat wouldn't scare them and told me to move so that they could prove it to me. I reminded them that I couldn't get out unless they got out of the way. They moved back down the tree; I got out, and then each of them tried it and *tremblingly* insisted that they weren't scared. None of them lasted out there as long as I had been forced to. It makes me angry that they wouldn't get out of my way when I was so terrified and wanted to come down!"

"Boys can be so thoughtless sometimes," says Dave, shaking his head down below.

"At least I think you grew out of that stage," Danielle reassures him.

"You *think* that I grew out of that stage?"

"Okay, you grew out of that stage."

You are now climbing precariously up a steep incline of branches. Just a few more feet ahead and Dave will be below you. You must be almost there. "Well, here we are." Danielle finds a comfortable place to sit off to the side. She tucks her skirt beneath her and points to two thick branches in front of you. They go straight up a few feet, straight out over nothing for a few more feet, and then bucket into the Freaky Seat, twining around one another all the way. Besides the fact that those two branches will be your only support, there is another disconcerting factor that you couldn't see from the ground below. One of the branches is completely dead and half-rotten. You look at Danielle. She is sitting, patiently waiting for you to try it.

(If you decide that she isn't worried, so a dead branch probably isn't a problem, go to page 100.)
(If you would like to ask some questions before trying it, go to page 111.)
(If you decide that now would be a good time to go to the Eagle's Nest, go to page 113.)

"Wait a minute, what are you doing?" Danielle sounds scared, but you can't look back to see. Once you turned yourself around in the Freaky Seat and began to climb out and up to the canopy branches, you had your back to her.

"Wow, cool! We never thought of that!" Dave shouts, observing what you are doing from below. The branches of the canopy above are so flimsy that your feet don't really have a place to step up. With your feet on the two spindly ends of the branches of the Freaky Seat, you lock your arms firmly into the mass of the canopy as your feet slip off the branches. Hanging there from a swinging, snapping mass of tangled branches over 30 feet of empty space, you wonder if this was really such a good idea. You hear a faint gasp from Danielle. "Danny, don't worry; I'm coming up!" Dave calls. You cannot look in the direction of his voice. Your arms are firmly locked, but your feet struggle to find the spindly branches that they slipped from. You find them again, propel yourself higher into the tangle and then slip again. Your arms are getting tired. You are now too high to reach the branches of the Freaky Seat, and you feel tied down on all sides. You lift your knee up and jab it into a mass of tangles, hoping that it will hold, then you push both arms up and part the branches and leaves above you like a swimmer breaking through the surface of the water. Blue sky appears. You wiggle up through the hole that you have made and pull and push yourself up through and out onto a carpet of leaves. The first thing that you realize is that nothing is solid up here. Everything gives or quakes. The only reason that the canopy can support your weight at all is because there is so much of it. The sunlight is blinding and all around you.

You gasp from your prostrate position. The view really is breathtaking! Goliath is the tallest tree around. You can see the blue of Lake Victoria in the distance on three sides of you. The tops of the other trees are everywhere but always below. Tiny houses and one-story buildings are visible here and there on the outskirts of the forest.

You lean back, shift a few poking branches and find yourself in a pretty comfortable position. From this posture you can hear snatches of Dave and Danielle's conversation.

"…going up too."

"…almost fell…."

Then you hear a strange "nyacking" noise. You sit up again and realize that you are not quite as much of a pioneer as you thought. A monkey is crouched about eight feet away looking more surprised to see you than you are to see it. It makes the same, "nyack, nyack!" noise.

You remember Dave's instructions about monkeys. "If you see a monkey, pick up a stick, don't act scared, and walk away. If you are in a tree, get out of it! Monkeys are dangerous. They can sit up to four feet tall and have killer teeth. They also spread rabies and AIDS."

You begin to think to yourself. "Dave said that if I am in a tree, I should get out of it." The monkey bares its teeth and snarls at you. "Or should I pick up a stick first? I shouldn't act like I am scared," you rehearse to yourself. You are startled when the monkey makes an even louder and angrier noise. This is a 40-foot tree and there is no quick way down. If you rush back the way you came, Dave will probably be blocking the way back across the Freaky Seat; after all, he said that he was coming too. Then the monkey would be able to bite you easily. You could race across the canopy and hope to find another way down.

Perhaps you could make it to another tree. You wonder how far away the Eagle's Nest is. The canopy, however, is monkey territory. The monkey is likely to know it better. Besides, he doesn't have to be afraid of falling through. Perhaps if you picked up a stick, it would intimidate the monkey long enough for you to warn Dave and Danielle that you're coming back down. You might be able to defend yourself against one monkey, but then again, how dangerous is one monkey?

(If you plunge back through the opening, go to page 117.)
(If you pick up a stick to defend yourself, go to page 120.)
(If you try to escape across the canopy, go to page 124.)

The liquid pools in droplets on your glasses as the snake slides quickly away. You hear your name being called. You wipe your glasses and then crawl away toward the sound of your name. "Are you all right?" Dave looks concerned.

"Yes," you answer.

"You didn't get bitten?"

"No, but the snake sprayed something all over my glasses."

"Did you touch any of it?"

"Well, yeah. I cleaned my glasses off!"

"Don't rub your eyes, whatever you do!" Dave warns.

You're about to say, "I could have guessed that," but he keeps talking.

"Boy, am I glad that I got out of there right away; I'm not wearing protective goggles! Those glasses probably saved your vision. Spitting cobra poison can be blinding. Anyway, let's go home. We shouldn't have been crawling around in those woods without a dog, anyway."

When you get home, his parents forbid any brush explorations without Simba because of your close call. Being that close to a black-necked spitting cobra with no defending dog is not something to be chanced again.

THE END

You begin your precarious venture. The two branches wiggle as you pull yourself up onto the flat part. Ahead you see the bucket of the Freaky Seat. Below you could see a very short and white-faced Dave, if you look down. "You can do it!" he calls. Anyone with a fear of heights would be very frightened at this point.

Slowly you turn yourself on your stomach 180 degrees. You could just slide forward on your stomach and plop down into the bucket headfirst, but you would rather proceed with your feet. Now, unfortunately, with your feet toward the bucket, you can't see where you are going. You inch backward face down, trying not to concentrate on the ground until you feel the branches drop out below you, then you slowly lower yourself, one leg on either side, straddling the seat. It is like sitting on a very narrow horse with two backbones and no stirrups. Holding onto the neck of the horse, you can now see Danielle, the pallor leaving her face. She is cheering.

"You did it!" Dave shouts from below. The distance to the ground *does* look a lot farther than it did when you looked up at the seat from the ground. Still, you have completed the challenge of the Freaky Seat! Looking around behind you, you get an idea. The two branches are attached up into the canopy, a tangle of live branches, dead branches and the roots of hanging vines, above the jungle floor. You are sure that Dave and Danielle have never gone farther than the Freaky Seat before. If you climbed up the other side of the Freaky Seat, you might be able to climb up the branches and push your way through. Dave and Danielle did say that the Eagle's Nest was one way to get up onto the canopy, but Goliath is the tallest tree around. Goliath's canopy is sure to be higher. A part of you longs to see what lies beyond the tangle of branches, but the branches you are on shrink considerably before they join the canopy. Will they hold your weight? And after you get up on the canopy, what then? The canopy will be a whole new realm of adventure or danger.

(If you decide to blaze a way to the new frontier of Goliath's canopy, go to page 93.)
(If you deem the whole idea an unsafe whim and would rather experience the canopy in proven safety, go to page 113.)

"We've got to get your eyes washed out!" Dave heaves you to your feet. "Desperate times call for desperate measures. Get on my back." You're in too much pain to argue. You can't see on the ride back, but you can tell that Dave is running as fast as he can. When Dave reaches his house, he races you to the sink. As soon as his parents find out what happened, his mother gives you eyedrops while his father radios for a plane to take you to the city for treatment.

Moments later Uncle Darryl gives a shout of jubilation. "Someone is on the radio at 3 in the afternoon! Not only that, but there is a mission plane in the air that will be flying over us in just a few minutes. The pilot has agreed to abort the flight and pick you up. Everybody pack quickly! God is looking out for us." He looks in your direction. "Specifically you."

You are happy to hear that a plane is on the way. You'd like to be out of pain as soon as possible.

By the time that you are driven out to the runway, the pain is lessening. The five of you fly out with the pilot in the little six-seater plane that they chartered. You are aware of the feel of flying in a way that you never were before when you could see, and you soon feel sick to your stomach.

The drive from the Mwanza airport to the hospital is terrible. The road is bumpy and full of potholes, and you can't see. The family warns you when the large bumps and potholes approach so that you can be prepared to be jostled all over the car, but they can't warn you about everything.

In the hospital your eyes are thoroughly cleaned out and bandaged. That evening you see light again for the first time since you saw the jets of venom. Your vision continues to improve in your time in the hospital. It looks like your left eye will fully recover. Your right eye may take longer, but you are not expected to have any lifetime difficulties with it. Dave blames himself for leaving without warning you about spitting cobras. You blame yourself for not following his example and getting away immediately. Dave has another thought. "If we had stayed to play with those kids, this wouldn't have happened; but don't consider this a punishment for not wanting to stay. We were under no obligation to."

You know that, and you're glad you were able to get to a hospital so quickly. You just wish this hadn't happened.

THE END

Dave helps you find your feet again. "Okay, here come some bushes; just push right through them. There's another root at your feet; don't trip! I see a road ahead. It's our driveway! Good, almost there. Now, when we get there I want you to try to run. I'll guide you around the turns." He grabs your arm. "Let's go!"

Now that you can't see, your other senses have become more sensitive. The driveway is sandy and gives with every step. Running without being able to see would be bad enough in a familiar place. As it is, the pain in your eyes drives you on. The ground is relatively flat, and then suddenly your right foot slips into a hole. "That's just a tire rut," Dave says, "and here comes Simba; so don't be surprised if you sense a large animal nearby. Simba, move!" You can tell that the dog must be blocking your path. You hear a grunt from Dave and a dragging sound as well as a dog whining. You conclude that the dog has been moved and keep going. The pain from your eyes is making your head ache, and you just wish that it would go away. Running feet approach. "Dave, what…?" It's Danielle.

"Spitting-cobra-both-eyes-get-Mom-and-Dad," Dave says in one breath.

The running feet fade away. By the time that Dave is directing you on how to get up onto the porch, you can hear the radio on inside. Aunt Debbie's voice greets you from the doorway. "Tilt your head back and hold one eye open." This is difficult because all that your pained eyes want to do is to stay shut. "Now the other eye. Good. Start blinking. Uncle Darryl is radioing for a plane to take you to Mwanza Hospital. We'll all come with you. Meanwhile, you need to start splashing water on your eyes. We've got to get as much of the venom out as possible."

If I can just find the bathroom, you think. Another moment tells you that Dave is still there, guiding you to the kitchen sink. The burning pain of the next step, eye rinsing, is something that you don't ever want to experience again.

"When will I be able to see again?" you want to know.

"I'm not sure," says Aunt Debbie.

Does that mean never? you wonder.

"Danielle, go look up spitting cobras in the snake book. I'm going to check my medical book to see if anything else should be done." You hear Dave describing the snake to Danielle in the next room. Footsteps approach. By now you can tell Danielle's footsteps from the rest of the family.

"Danny, tell me what the snake book says!" you plead. "I've got to know whether my eyes are going to recover or not!"

"Dave says that it was a black-necked spitting cobra. The book says that its venom can cause temporary or permanent blindness."

"Great. So we really *don't* know."

"How hard were you hit?" Danielle asks.

"Pretty hard," you reply, knowing that it's the truth.

"We'll keep praying," Danielle says with hope. "God has been known to perform miracles before. We've seen them around here."

Uncle Darryl tries to radio the nearest city, Mwanza, but finds out that no one is on the receiving radio. He then tries to get through to the missionaries in Dodoma, another Tanzanian city. They happen to be on the radio. Dodoma and Mwanza are connected by phone lines, so Uncle Darryl waits a second hour while the missionary in Dodoma tries to get a call through to the missionary in Mwanza. Two and a half hours from the time that Uncle Darryl began the process, the missionary in Mwanza calls him on the radio. Uncle Darryl gives her the details of your injury and explains that all of you will need a plane. She calls the pilot's home. The pilot's wife answers the phone and explains that he took two of their kids to the pool at a hotel that afternoon. She had a cold and couldn't go. The coordinator then calls the hotel. The pilot gets his two kids out of the pool, dried off and dressed. He drives home, puts on his uniform, and drives out to the airport. Four and a half hours after Uncle Darryl turned on the radio, the news arrives that the pilot is on his way in a little six-seater plane.

Uncle Darryl is delighted. "That was God's providence. We got a response to a radio message sent in the afternoon, *and* they had a plane and pilot available! It only took 4 hours and 30 minutes for the pilot to be on his way."

It's hard for you to feel optimistic right now.

Aunt Debbie agrees with Uncle Darryl. "That might be a record time for getting out a radio call. Not only that, the phone lines were working between Mwanza and Dodoma. Incredible!"

Working? you wonder. *It took an hour to make one phone call!* Aunt Debbie continues, "Any longer, and we would have had to wait until tomorrow to fly. Planes don't like to land after dark here."

"Is it getting dark?" you want to know.

"A bit." Aunt Debbie remembers that you can't see. "The sunset will start soon."

Will you ever see a sunset again? you wonder.

"Isn't it great? In exactly one more hour, you'll be in the hospital!" Dave is exultant.

This family's exuberance is starting to get to you.

"You mean that the plane will arrive in Mwanza in one hour," Danielle clarifies. "We won't be to the hospital until at least half an hour after that. If the staff isn't there, we might still have to wait until tomorrow."

"No, we won't." Dave is determined. "This is an emergency. We'll drag the medical staff over in their bathrobes if we have to."

"I think that the missionaries in Mwanza will inform the medical staff for us. Those people go to an awful lot of trouble to take care of us. It's already 6 p.m., so the sun is beginning to go down. That plane better get here quickly." The pain in your eyes has subsided a little bit.

By the time the plane arrives, you still can't see. The family has packed quickly for you and for themselves. They are ready to go. You close your eyes as the pilot prays for a safe trip and that you will regain your sight. As you open your eyes from the prayer, you see a glimmer of pink light shining through your left eye.

You can barely make out the forms of the plane and the people. You will not be permanently blind! The sunset, or what you can see of it, is gorgeous. You wonder if you've ever felt happier.

All of you board the plane in jubilation. Through your time in the hospital, your eyes continue to improve. When you finally leave to return to your home country, you know that you will recover. It was a mistake to look back at the snake; but God has restored your sight, and you are grateful for that.

The End

"Danny, would you climb out on this Freaky Seat? I mean…."

"Not on your life," she replies with conviction.

As it is your life you are concerned about, you try another tactic. "When you last climbed out to the Freaky Seat, was this branch dead?"

"Probably," Danielle supposes, "but that was a couple of years ago. The bark might have still been on it, so we couldn't tell. Nobody's forcing you."

"What's taking so long?" yells the little midget looking up from far below you.

"Dave!" you call back, "would you have challenged me to climb out on the Freaky Seat if you had known that one of the branches was dead?"

"Sure," he replies.

"Would you climb out on it?"

"Sure I would! I've done it plenty of times. But for now, I think I'd better stay down here below you just to show you how high up you are."

"He's scared." Danielle shifts uncomfortably.

"Am not! Just waiting in case of the event that I have to catch our little friend! Don't worry, even if the branch does break (which I really doubt that it will), there are two of them, and both are attached up into the canopy as well as to the tree."

You wonder if he is actually waiting to catch you, but from the nonchalance in his stance he doesn't seem to be expecting to. You now have all the information. The final choice is up to you.

(If you are going to try the challenge, go to page 100.)
(If you would rather do something else, go to page 113.)

A small amount of walking from Goliath finds the four of you (Simba included) standing at the base of a tree only about two-thirds as tall as Goliath. The tree seems to have two trunks that twist around each other enabling you to climb them. "The Eagle's Nest is at the top of the next tree over," Dave explains. "That tree, as you can see," he points to it, "has a straight trunk and no branches until you get about ten feet up. We climb up this tree first and then cross the Bridge to get to that one." The Bridge, you find out, is a thick wooden vine hanging between the two trees. Danielle has already begun to cross it, balancing on the vine below like a tightrope walker while holding on to the canopy above her head. She makes it across and Dave follows. You find that as long as you are holding on firmly to the branches above you, crossing the Bridge vine is a cinch. You wouldn't want to cross it without the handholds, though; it sways. Danielle and Dave are now climbing the taller tree ahead of you. They push themselves through a small hole in the canopy branches at the top of the tree and disappear. You push yourself through the same hole and find yourself in the sunlight.

Danielle and Dave have already begun to get comfortable in their favorite places. The area definitely looks like a bright green nest. You find that it is not an easy task with all of the twigs poking through the leaves to get comfortable. You pull yourself into the nest, find a larger branch to sit on below the leaves and look over the nest rim. The view is beautiful. The tops of trees are everywhere with Lake Victoria and its islands in the distance in front of you. You are unable to see any distance behind you, due to taller trees blocking your view.

"Wait a minute." Danielle is staring into the foliage of the side of the nest. "What's *that?*" Dave leans to look over her shoulder.

"I think it's an animal. Unless it's some kind of furry mold or fungus growth on the tree." You crawl across the nest to get a look too. It doesn't look like a growth to you. It looks like a gray, furry creature. You can see a long skinny tail and arms wrapped around an enormous head. It has its back to you.

"Do you think it's a monkey?" Danielle asks somewhat fearfully.

"No, it's not a monkey; it's got big ears. Look!" Dave stares confusedly then gets an inspiration. "I'll bet it's a bush baby! We'll know if we see its eyes. Let's wake him up!"

"No, let 'im sleep. He's so cute!" Danielle croons. "Besides, bush babies are nocturnal, so they sleep during the day. Their large eyes help them see at night."

"How did you know *that?*" Dave glances back at her.

"Remember when Mom had us do animal reports last year? I did mine on bush babies."

"Oh, yeah, that was when I did leopards," Dave remembers.

All three of you huddled on a little area of the Eagle's Nest proves to be too much of a strain for one of the branches. It cracks loudly. The bush baby turns over in its nest, blinks its large eyes and then leaps away through the tree branches like a frog. You notice that its feet have thumbs, but that's all that you have time to notice. The animal is gone in an instant.

"Wow!" Danielle lets out a breath and laughs, "That was great! I always wanted to see one of those. Wasn't it adorable?"

"I thought it was ugly," Dave admits honestly. Danielle tosses her head.

"Everyone is entitled to their own tastes, I suppose." You have found a comfortably shaded position against the side of the nest. Dave looks about ready to fall asleep in a makeshift canopy bed. He has pulled his baseball cap over his eyes. Danielle, sitting in the glaring sun, is trying to find a shady spot. She finally gives up.

"You guys, I'm getting sunburned; can I trade places with one of you?" Dave looks like he's sleeping, so you agree to trade. The equatorial sun is definitely hot. You begin to long for the deliciously shady cool of the woods below. Danielle seems to feel the same way. Simba whines from the ground. "Dave," Danielle calls softly. "I think we should go home now." There is no response. "Dave!" she tries again. "DAVE!"

"Wha…what?" Dave rouses quickly, nearly losing his baseball cap. He puts it back on and groans sleepily.

On the way back across the Bridge, Dave is so drowsy he looks like he might fall off. He *does* lose his hat, which wakes him up a bit. On the way home, however, his grumping proves that he is indeed waking up from his nap. But when you four arrive home, he is just as excited to relate the story of the unusual bush baby sighting as you and Danielle are.

THE END

"Dave! There's a monkey; I'm coming back down!" you shout as you lower yourself back down through the hole in the canopy. You feel your feet guided to the branches below. You hear Dave's voice muttering behind you. "I pray to God that these branches can hold *two* people." You slowly bring yourself down and then begin to crawl backwards across the Freaky Seat branches after Dave. You are trying to go as quickly as you can, but the danger of falling from this high above the ground is very real. You drop down into the Freaky Seat. Once you find it, you turn around and look for the others. Dave is almost off the Freaky Seat's two branches, and Danielle is already halfway down the tree. You start to rise from your sitting position and hear a long low "Crraaaccck."

Dave jumps onto the main branch of the tree. "Hurry!"

You pull yourself onto the flat part of the seat, turn 180 degrees on your stomach and go feet first down and off the Freaky Seat branches. You didn't expect when you first got slowly onto that seat how quickly you would be coming off it! You've made it off the branches of the Freaky Seat, and neither branch appears to be broken. Dave has already begun making his way down the tree. You follow, trying to remember the order in which you place your feet. Now you have to do it backwards.

Finally you reach the ground. All three of you are shaking. It feels wonderful to be on something solid. Danielle speaks first.

"I thought I heard monkeys, so I started to climb down while Dave waited to help you."

"There was only one monkey," you clarify.

"Are you sure that there was only one?" Dave asks, pointing up to the tree behind you.

Monkeys by the dozen are coming, jumping and swinging through the trees. They begin to play and "nyack" angrily at the three of you on the ground. "Aren't you glad that we're not still up there? Let's get out of here! Simba," Dave fondly pets the dog who has just arrived. "So you finally finished off the badger?"

"There is no way that Simba could finish off a badger," Danielle says with conviction.

"We need to leave," Dave requests. "We can't climb trees around here any more." Upon the arrival of the dog, the monkeys seem to have quieted down somewhat. The four of you return home. Dave says that he would like to explore Goliath's canopy sometime when the monkeys aren't there. Danielle thinks that maybe for the sake of the view from the canopy she'll board the Freaky Seat again sometime way in the future when there are no more monkeys, but she's not sure.

THE END

You pull a stick out of the dead mass below the leaves of the canopy and crouch by the exit hole. "Dave! Danny! There's a monkey up here! Get out of the tree, now!"

"I knew that was a monkey!" Danielle's voice comes floating up.

"You'd better come down; a monkey can be dangerous. Is it acting strangely?" Dave asks. Unless you are a wildlife specialist or a longtime resident, how are you supposed to know that? You turn back around, brandishing your stick, hoping to hold off the monkey for long enough that Dave can get out of your way. Suddenly your blood freezes.

"Dave, now there are four up here! Are you out of my way?"

Dave's voice comes back up through the opening, once again from very close. "Four! You'd better get moving, pronto!" You look down the hole at Dave's face peering up through the hole.

"You're still in my way!"

"I'll help you down; come on! Don't look afraid."

You already look frightened. "Now there are seven! They're running toward me!"

No matter how hard you try, you can't keep the fear off your face when seven monkeys appear and then run at you with sharp teeth bared. You come back through that hole so fast that you don't have time to think about the 35 feet of empty space below. Dave grabs your feet, plants them securely on the branches and then turns around in the Freaky Seat to flee out the other side. "Hurry!"

Danielle, who has already made it to the ground, yells with fear in her voice, "They're coming!" As you lower yourself into the Freaky Seat, you see dozens of African vervet monkeys of all sizes swinging toward you. "Oh, great. We're no match for them, especially up here, and they know it. Don't act like you're afraid, and keep climbing down." You're crossing the Freaky Seat branches quickly over 30 feet of empty space; 30 African vervet monkeys are swinging toward you with bared teeth; and you aren't supposed to show any fear? Good night!

You start to laugh hysterically as you turn your back on the monkeys and climb up and over the other side of the Freaky Seat. As you do the 180-degree turn to get off the branches feet first, you see that the monkeys have stopped their pursuit. Perhaps not showing fear has something to it after all.

You and Dave begin descending the tree at a potentially unhealthy but incredibly fast pace. Then the monkeys begin their chase again. The ground is rapidly getting closer, but so are they and then, "Arrarrarrarrarrarrarrarruff!" The monkeys flee back up the tree. You and Dave land on the ground amidst the joyous leaping and licking of Simba.

"Simba!" Dave puts his arms around the neck of the dog, who begins joyously licking his face, knocking the baseball cap askew. Danielle grins.

"Dave doesn't normally let her do that. But I guess that letting your dog slobber all over your face is a fair reward when she saved your hide. Even though dogs can't climb trees, monkeys are terrified of them. As soon as Simba arrived at the base of the tree, wow! You should've seen those monkeys run!"

"I did," you remind her.

"I know; it's just an expression."

Dave looks up at you with wet hair plastered all over his forehead. "Next time," he says, "just come down right away. Don't wait for 12 monkeys to appear."

"I didn't. I picked up a stick so that I could hold off the one monkey and warn the two of you!"

"That might have worked," Dave concedes, "if it had been only one monkey."

"You guys, let's go home. That was a close call, and I feel like going back to a nice safe house and yard. Besides, we can't go to the Eagle's Nest now, not with all these monkeys around!" says Danielle persuasively.

"Yeah," Dave agrees. "Let's go home."

The End

You stand up on the shaking canopy and then dash off to the side.

You feel both legs go through the leaves. As you sink tangled into the canopy, you grab anything within reach. The canopy is not as solid as it looked. Few places can hold your weight. You hear Danielle's scream as your blue jeans appear below. "Don't let go! There's nothing beneath you!" You had assumed that from the feel of emptiness. It's not so bad, though. With your head and arms above the canopy and the rest of you below, it is impossible to look down.

"I'm coming up!" shouts Dave.

"No, wait!" You struggle to pull yourself up through the canopy, but the fact that you're holding on to a bunch of little sticks and vines and kicking at thin air doesn't help much. Dave's head appears through the canopy hole. He looks your direction and

laughs. "Slipped off the edge, did you? Let's see if I can get you out of there." He begins to pull himself on his stomach across the canopy and then stops. "Oh, wow. I'm surprised that you got that far out! The tree drops off back here. What were you doing, running? Anyway, Danny thought that she heard a monkey, so we need to get out of this tree." You point in the direction of the monkey. Dave turns around to see eight of them sitting and watching the two of you.

"Oh, great!" Dave starts talking very fast. "So *that's* why you ran. Why did you run this way, anyway? Forget where the hole was? Oh, Lord God, help us! And please help me to find some way to get my friend out of this tree before 8, excuse me, 12 monkeys attack us. Amen. Well, 8 or 12, you're still God." He seems comforted. Now there are 14 monkeys.

"What to do, what to do? Danny, we'll need your help up here! Danny!"

"I'm coming!"

"Hurry!"

"I'm crossing the Freaky Seat!" She sounds affronted.

"Well, don't fall, just come quickly!"

You stop counting monkeys at 30. Some are beginning to play. Some sit watching you, some are tiny, some are enormous; but none of them crosses a seemly invisible barrier that must be protecting you.

Danielle appears, white-faced. She gasps at the sight of all the monkeys.

"I've prayed," Dave reassures her. "Thin ice method; hold onto my feet; we've got to get our guest out of the tree."

"I've prayed too. But what if you fall through the tree? No, I'll let God take care of that too." She firmly grabs the soles of his shoes and shuts her eyes. Dave's pushing himself across the deceptively thin branches does resemble a rescue on ice in a cold climate. You're glad that he's coming, because though you have a good grip in the thin vines and branches, your arms are getting tired. He stretches out his hands to reach you. Danielle's arms are fully extended as well.

"Come on!" he coaxes. "You'll have to let go!" You firmly secure one hand in the vines and then untangle and stretch out the other. He grabs it. The second hand is relatively easy. "Okay, Danny, you pull, I'll try to wiggle backwards." Danielle opens her eyes and pulls, but Dave has no time to try to wiggle backward. He shoots backward toward the exit hole in the canopy, pulling you out of your hole and back with him. Even the quivery part of the canopy near the exit feels stable after what you have just been hanging from. Danielle has already started down. Dave grins. "I have a strong sister."

"It comes from climbing trees, hauling rocks and paddling!" Danielle calls up. "And from adrenaline," she adds more quietly. The monkeys are still there.

Dave climbs down through the hole and out across the Freaky Seat. You follow. Even the Freaky Seat seems stable now. You see the sunlight streaming through the hole you made in the canopy, and you are glad that you were unable to look down. When the three of you reach the ground, Simba is waiting for you, obviously having abandoned whatever animal she had cornered before. As soon as the three of you hit the ground, the monkeys rush all over Goliath. Simba barks excitedly at the base of the tree, scaring them higher up into it. They "nyack" angrily at her.

"That was a miracle," says Danielle, looking up.

"Yup," Dave agrees. "Monkeys just sitting there and not bothering us after we had invaded their territory!"

"No, I meant that I was actually able to cross the Freaky Seat and beyond; can you believe that?" Danielle says, still gazing upwards at the seat of branches.

"Well, that too," Dave concedes. "We couldn't have done what we did without you." He pauses. "Come on, you guys; let's go home."

The End

Your eyes immediately begin to sting and then to burn. "Dave!" you scream, crawling blindly off into the direction that you know the snake isn't, only to find yourself tangled in that bush again. You hear him calling your name. You yell again, and soon you hear his voice very close.

"Were you bitten? Are you okay? What's wrong with your eyes?" You tell him. You can't see his reaction, but his next words clarify it. "Come on! We have to get your eyes cleaned out as soon as we can. Blink; get your eyes to water." Blindly you are pulled behind him through the brush. You are in serious pain, and you can't see anything. "Maybe I should leave you here and bring water to you. That might be faster. No. I would have to go and come back, and that would take too much time. I'll guide you, but we have to hurry. Duck! Go to your right. There's a root…." You trip.

(If you weigh less than 101 pounds, go to page 102.)
(If you weigh more than 100 pounds, go to page 105.)

You watch as Danielle and Dave ascend the hill to the pastor's house, leaving you and Simba by the edge of the woods. You are holding tightly to Simba's collar with one hand. It soon becomes clear that the dog is determined to get to the pastor's house. She strains and pulls and drags you forward. You grip her collar firmly with both hands and hook your feet to a tree root, making it impossible for the large Rhodesian Ridgeback to drag you any farther. Finally the dog stops straining and lies down on the ground. You relax but keep both sweaty hands on her collar.

In a flash the dog pulls through your fingers and begins bounding up the hill. You weren't prepared for that much force exerted that quickly. You run up the hill after the dog. By the time you reach the back of the house, you have lost her. Hearing voices, you follow them around to the front of the house. Danielle and Dave are sitting on little wooden folding chairs drinking water from plastic mugs. The hostess, probably the pastor's wife, is standing nearby, and Danielle is speaking. They all look at you. You are out of breath, but a squawking of chickens around the back of the house tells all. Dave is up in a moment, thrusts a sloshing cup at Danielle and runs around the back of the house, leaving her to explain the situation. The situation, however, explains itself. First, the pastor's large red rooster comes tearing around the house. Then Simba appears, bounding in all the glory of the hunt. Finally Dave, running as though his legs are falling off, rounds the bend and disappears behind the house and down the hill.

The pastor's wife, a large, middle-aged woman, looks seriously worried. She runs off after Dave. Danielle stands up, setting their cups down on her wooden folding chair. "We'd better go too; Simba can be hard to corner sometimes." All four of you begin a game at the bottom of the hill. Like a quarterback with a football, Simba, with the rooster in her mouth, is ducking and dodging around the four of you. Dave does a flying leap and catches the dog around the neck. The surprised dog drops the rooster, who begins to hobble away. Simba drags Dave a few feet trying to get the rooster.

"Stop!" Dave commands. Simba stops. "Good dog!" Dave congratulates her. She lunges for the

rooster again. "Stop!" yells Dave. The procedure is repeated. Finally Simba stops lunging altogether and sits down. "It's about time that someone started training this dog!" Dave commends himself. The pastor's wife then directs a question at Danielle. Danielle looks hurriedly around.

"Where is the rooster?" she asks. While watching Dave train the dog, you, Danielle, and the pastor's wife forgot all about it.

It must have wandered away. While Dave holds Simba, the three of you search the bushes and the woods around there. There is no sign of the rooster. Then Danielle holds Simba while the rest of you search the yard and the neighbors' yards.

Then Dave gets a brilliant idea. "How about we let Simba find the rooster?"

"Yes!" Danielle agrees. "She's good at finding things. That's how I found you guys earlier; I told Simba to smell you out!"

"Okay." Dave takes the collar back from Danielle. "Simba, find the chicken! Find the rooster!"

"She doesn't know what you're telling her to do!" Danielle is sure that that is why Simba won't move. "Just walk her around the area and see if she sniffs at anything." Simba sniffs at *everything*. Dave's training seems to have had some effect, however. She won't go near any chickens. "This is great!" Dave is excited. "It worked! My training worked! She has learned not to chase chickens any more."

"She also won't be much help in finding the rooster." Danielle is crestfallen. You four searchers then pray for guidance to find the rooster. How far can a wounded bird go?

The sun is beginning to go down. Crickets are beginning to chirp from the bushes around the house. "It's almost 5:30. We need to go home." Danielle looks tired. The three of you say good-bye and give your sincerest apologies to the pastor's wife, who looks pretty tired too. Danielle promises to replace the chicken, though the pastor's wife is highly skeptical that Danielle will be able to find a rooster as big as the one that was lost. "Large chickens depend on a large rooster," Danielle explains as the four of you, including the dog, walk sadly home. "If she can't get another large rooster, all the chicks will be puny and small."

"We'll do the best we can," Dave assures her.

The next day brings good news. Later that evening, after the four of you (including the dog) went away, the rooster hobbled home. The pastor's family did not lose their prize chicken! Simba has now been officially banned from any future visits.

THE END

"I'd like to go up with Danny," you say. "Simba looks pretty determined to get up there, and she's more likely to obey Dave, her owner, than me, a stranger."

"Probably," Danielle agrees with you. "Let's go."

"Hurry!" Dave begs. You and Danielle climb up the hill.

"*Hodi!*" Danielle calls as she reaches the top of the hill and walks around to the front of the house.

"*Dani! Karibu. Karibu sana!*" A large middle-aged woman who you gather must be the pastor's wife greets you.

"*Shikamo.*" Danielle shakes her hand and curtsies. "All girls have to curtsy when greeting an older person," Danielle quickly explains to you.

The pastor's wife replies to the greeting with "*Marahaba*" and continues talking. "*Subiri, nipate viti, kwa wewe na rafiki yako. Huyu ni nani?"* Danielle introduces you to her. She seems pleased. *"Unataka chai? Au maji kama kawaida?"*

"Maji tafadhali," Danielle answers. She turns to you. *"Na wewe, unataka chai au maji?"* She translates. "Would you like water or tea? Say water; tea will take longer and we're trying to get back down to Dave!"

"Water, please," you say obligingly.

"Anataka maji," Danielle explains to the pastor's wife. The pastor's wife bustles off and produces two wooden folding chairs. After the two of you are seated, she walks back into her house, presumably to get water. She returns moments later carrying two plastic cups with handles full of water, cool from being in the house. You each take one. Danielle and the pastor's wife start into a conversation. Danielle translates periodically. Her eyes shine with delight as she gives you the pastor's wife's latest report. "She says that her husband took the Kizinza/Kiswahili Scripture tract to the home of some of his (the pastor's) Wazinza friends. They read through both sides (the Kiswahili translation side and the Kizinza translation side), argued over it and in the end asked to receive Christ! She said that the Scripture tract is a great tool for the church to use when evangelizing among the Wazinza people. Wait till I tell Mom and Dad! She also said that her husband has been enjoying the

books we brought for him. Some people in our home church got together some biblical materials, like a Bible concordance, a dictionary (in English, of course), an atlas…. Her husband would also like 50 copies of the tract to use for teaching Christian basics. Hmm….”

Danielle and the pastor's wife finally get to a point in the discussion where Danielle motions toward the back of the house and down the hill. You assume that she is explaining about Dave and Simba. The pastor's wife seems relieved; you assume that it is because the dog is being held in check. There are chickens everywhere in the yard. Danielle stands up to take her leave. You each return your cups; Danielle curtsies again; good-byes are said; and the two of you walk back to Dave.

When you reach the edge of the hill, you are surprised. Dave is still holding and reprimanding a straining dog; however, the dog is no longer trying to get to the pastor's house. Simba is trying to go to the right and down the path that runs along the base of the hill.

“I can't understand it!” Dave explains. “Halfway through the time you were up there, Simba just switched directions!”

“Maybe one of the pastor's chickens wandered down the hill,” Danielle suggests.

Dave is skeptical. "It would have to be a pretty big chicken, seeing as though she'd rather have this one than a whole yard full!"

"Yeah," Danielle agrees. "Well, give me the dog. I've explained everything to the pastor's wife already, so she'll probably be waiting up there with a cup of water for you. You won't have to explain how our mother is doing or discuss the weather or anything like that."

"Thanks, Danny. My arm hurts! Here you go; I won't be long." Dave hands over the dog's collar. Simba outsmarts the two of them, though. Right at the second when Dave is letting go and Danielle is starting to grab hold, Simba breaks free and takes off running down the path. "Oh, great! I shouldn't have let go until you had a firm hold on her. Here, I'll go get her." Dave turns to run down the path.

"No!" Danielle stops him. "You go get your water; we'll go get the dog. Come on!" she calls to you and dashes down the path at lighting speed. You follow her.

The dusty little path twists and turns through thick flower bushes. You can see Danielle rounding bends ahead of you. Suddenly she stops. You almost crash into her. Looking around at the path in front, you see Simba hopping around and barking at the largest porcupine that you have ever seen. "A South African Crested Porcupine!" Danielle is delighted.

"I've always wanted to see one of those! I've found the spines but never seen the animal before! I'll bet Simba hasn't either. Simba," she addresses the dog, "I wouldn't go near that thing if I were you!" The porcupine is indeed impressive. Some of its stripe-ringed quills are a foot long! It pads along nonchalantly and doesn't even seem to notice the dog hopping around it and barking. Seeing the two of you arriving, Simba decides not to prolong the hunt any more. She gets too close. "Yipe!" She backs off. The porcupine lumbers away, showing off its impressive coat of knitting needles, three of which are jabbed into the dog's muzzle.

"Why do you always have to learn the hard way?" Danielle asks the forlorn dog.

Simba trots off and begins rubbing her muzzle against a nearby tree. One of the quills falls out; the other two seem to have wedged themselves in deeper. "No, Simba, stop it! We need to get you home." Danielle holds out her hands. "Simba, come." The dog comes. Danielle pulls one quill out easily. Simba whines when she touches the other one. "I think I'll let my mom take care of that one." Danielle leaves the other two quills on the ground. "You're free to pick up the quills for souvenirs if you want to," she says to you, motioning toward the ground. "Somehow I don't feel like salvaging them."

"Hey, you guys!" Dave comes trotting around the bend. "Did you find Simba? Oh." Simba whines at him. "I see that she found a porcupine. Is it still around? I want to see it!"

Danielle sighs. "Somewhere around here, I guess. I didn't have time to grab Simba after she lunged for it. Maybe she learned something."

"Hold still." Dave is kneeling down in front of the dog, examining the remaining spine.

"What are you doing?" Danielle is indignant.

"Getting the quill out." Dave pulls quickly in the right direction. The dog yelps, but the spine comes free. "This is one big quill! I think I'll keep it."

Danielle shakes her head. "Suit yourself. Let's take Simba home to get her nose cleaned up." Danielle starts walking away.

Dave chuckles. "Nothing like a naughty dog for finding adventure." He turns to you. "So, did you get a good look at the porcupine? How big was it?"

THE END

"Simba! Simba!" you shout. The lizard tenses. Simba bursts back into the clearing. You can hear Dave and Danielle running frantically behind her. Simba growls and dives for the lizard's neck. At the same time the lizard flips its tail around and gashes Simba across the front legs. Simba yelps but then goes right back to fighting. "Oh, great," Dave says as he helplessly beholds the scene.

"She might not be able to kill this one! It's too big!" Danielle is panicking.

"Get sticks, we've got to help!" Dave rips a large branch off a nearby tree and runs at the lizard.

"Dave, jump!" Danielle screams. Without thinking, Dave jumps, narrowly missing the swinging tail.

"That was stupid!" Dave says as he runs back to the two of you. "Let's be more careful not to get that close." Simba is running around, jumping and dodging the heavy, sharp tail. She doesn't seem to be having fun any more. She yelps as she is hit again.

"We've got to get her away from here!" Danielle shouts, sobbing.

"Let's run away and call her with us," Dave suggests. The three of you race off through the brush, yelling Simba's name. Finally a crashing in the woods signals her arrival. Tail wagging, she runs up to Danielle and Dave. Danielle hugs her neck, sobbing with relief.

Dave speaks first. "That was one big lizard!" He pets Simba roughly on the head, and she yelps. He notices a cut line across the left side of her face. "Let's take Simba home."

"If only Simba wasn't so keen on killing reptiles!" Danielle sniffs. "She's killed a four-foot *kenge* before, but that last one was at least seven feet! She didn't have much of a chance."

"*Kenge* is the Kiswahili word for monitor lizard," Dave says to you, "and, by the way, Danny," he turns to her, "thanks for telling me to jump when you did. Don't mention my running at the lizard to Mom and Dad if you don't have to. I didn't get hurt, and I've learned my lesson. Let's just hope that we never get into a situation like that again."

"So," Danielle chuckles, "our safety system worked."

"What system, exactly?" you ask her.

"Dave and I have a system. When one of us gives an order and doesn't explain why, like when I told Dave to jump, the other follows through and asks questions later."

"Yes," says Dave to you. "If a hawk were swooping at you right now, I would tell you to 'duck.' By the time I said, 'A hawk is swooping toward you so duck,' it would have gotten you already."

You wonder exactly what that means.

Danielle explains, "A hawk got stuck in my hair once 'cause I didn't duck fast enough. That's why we set up this system of obedience."

Your arrival at home is met with great concern from the parents. Aunt Debbie cleans up Simba's wounds while the rest of you run for whatever supplies she needs. Simba just loves the attention. You, Dave, and Danielle agree to avoid that area of the brush from now on.

THE END

You stand frozen, staring into the beady little eyes of the giant reptile. It gets a bored look on its face, turns its neck away from you and lumbers off through the undergrowth. You wonder if it will come back, but it doesn't. Soon you can't hear it any more. You hear Dave calling your name and the sound of them coming back your way. Dave comes into the clearing, followed by Danielle who is holding on to Simba. Simba goes and sniffs excitedly at the animal's burrow. "Maybe we should take Simba away; there might be a monitor lizard in there," Danielle suggests.

"There was," you manage to say. "It crawled out of the burrow after I walked by."

"How big was it?" Dave wants to know.

"The body was about three feet," you remember. "With the head and the tail, maybe seven feet?" Dave whistles.

"Wow," Danielle seems impressed. Dave goes and peers into the burrow. "Most of it is dark, but, yes, a pretty big lizard could fit in here."

"Let's go before it comes back!" Danielle sounds slightly panicked. "Simba always attacks reptiles, and one with a tail that big could really hurt her!"

"Let's go," Dave agrees.

A short walk later, Simba picks up on another scent. "We must be getting near the airstrip," Danielle comments. She is still holding on to Simba's collar. Sure enough, moments later you can see a large grassy airstrip through the trees with Lake Victoria on the other side of it. Simba pulls Danielle toward a clump of gnarly brush trees. The area under the trees is sprinkled with white feathers. In the center of the clump of trees, a large white bird is fluttering and flopping around. It's about a foot and a half long. "An egret," Danielle labels it. "It looks like it caught its foot in some string that someone threw away under this tree."

"Unfortunately, egrets are fish eaters. It would taste terrible." Dave grimaces.

"Dave!" Danielle sounds affronted. "Here, take Simba and give me your pocketknife." Dave produces a pocketknife from a case on his belt and takes the dog from Danielle.

"Simba's not really interested in the bird, any-way," he says to Danielle. As if to prove his point,

Simba lies down on the ground and turns her head the other way. The bird is terrified and flutters the other direction, but Danielle manages to cut the line free. The bird does not fly away.

"It must have injured itself when it was flapping around," says Danielle, looking concerned. "We'll have to take it home with us. It could get hurt out here, and it will certainly starve with no fish to eat."

"Danny, the animal lover," Dave comments. "Okay, Danny, pick it up and let's go."

"I'm not sure." Danielle looks nervous.

"You're not sure if you want to take it back to our house?" Dave asks.

"No," she replies. "I'm not sure if I want to pick it up."

"Come on, Danny, you're the one with pet chickens; pick it up!"

"Okay." Danielle quickly reaches for the bird from the back. It flips around and bites her hand. "Well!" says Danielle holding up a scratched index finger. "That's gratitude for you!"

"It was just scared. Here, let me try." Dave slowly reaches for the bird. It pecks at him a few times and then stops. Thumbs on top, his hands encircle the bird's wings, holding its long legs to its body while its head sticks out in front. He holds it out awkwardly. "Okay, let's go." Simba trots along curiously beside him. The bird doesn't like it and shivers.

Once you all make it home, and it is clear that Simba is not going to hurt the bird, you all decide to leave the bird out in the yard. Danielle talks about making the bird into a pet, temporarily, of course, but to no avail. Two hours after your arrival back at the missionary home, the bird slips away. It probably went down to the lake to catch some fish, but you never see it again.

THE END

You don't wait to see what the giant lizard will do; you run after the others. When you reach Dave, the last in line, you are winded and your heart is pounding. Off in the distance, all of you can hear the crackling of dead leaves. Simba sniffs the air and Danielle grabs her collar. Simba whines and pulls in the direction of the noise. Danielle looks down at the dog. "Judging from Simba's reaction, that was a reptile. She loves, or rather, hates reptiles and kills any she runs across. She killed a three-foot *kenge* once."

"And judging from your reaction," Dave grins at you, "it must have been a pretty big one. By the way, a *kenge* is a monitor lizard. Danielle slips into Kiswahili sometimes. So how big was this reptile?"

"Including the tail, about seven feet," you estimate. "It crawled out from under a tree behind me."

"Seven feet? Two meters?" Dave is laughing in surprise. "You're joking!"

Danielle has recovered from her original gaping expression when you related its length to her. "You're sure about that size?" You nod.

"It crawled out of its burrow and passed within a few feet of me."

"Whoa," Danielle shakes her head. "I'm glad I held on to Simba just then. She's killed *kenges* before, but that one might have hurt her. They have killer tails, and that one could probably do some real damage."

"It's probably good that you ran away," Dave affirms. "The thing could have slashed you with its tail, if it perceived you as a threat. Then, again, what could be a threat to a thing like that? Not an unarmed person, certainly."

There is a crackling and a crashing in the brush far away but definitely coming closer. "Is that it again?" Danielle asks with a twinge of fear. Simba whines. "Let's get out of here!" Danielle calls and starts running in the other direction with the dog. You and Dave, hearing the closer approach of whatever it is, run too.

Danielle lets go of Simba's collar, and the dog runs ahead, enjoying bounding over bushes. Soon all of you are leaping large bushes too. It's actually kind of fun. Finally the four of you stop, all out of breath except Simba, who is panting happily. You have made it to the edge of the woods. Up ahead loom larger trees. "Nothing seems to be following us," Dave observes and then chuckles. "The Horsie should be around here somewhere."

You push back a curtain of leaves and step into the woods, a lightly roofed area of tall leafy trees. "Here it is!" Danielle calls from some distance away. You and Dave follow her voice to a smaller tree with a large thick branch about six inches in diameter growing out from it. It grows straight out for about six or seven feet and then stops abruptly.

"This," Danielle shows you, "is the Horsie." She pushes on it with her hand. It bounces easily. "We try to keep our balance standing on that animal while someone else moves it around."

"It's hard," Dave admits. While all of you gathered around the Horsie talking, Simba has decided to take a nap underneath it.

"Simba," Danny speaks sternly. "If you don't move, you're going to be squashed!" Simba wags her tail but doesn't move.

"Come, Simba," Dave calls. Simba heaves herself up and walks over to him, swinging her tail. "Good dog!"

The three of you spend the rest of your day shaking the Horse for someone else as well as balancing and falling on a walking, trotting, cantering, galloping, and sometimes rodeo horse. Dave and Danny can balance pretty well on a walk, a slow up and down. A trot is a series of small jolts that they can handle for a fair amount of time. The canter consists of larger and bouncier up and down motions; they generally fall. Falling is not a big deal in the sandy, leafy dirt, unless, of course, the dog gets in the way. None of you can handle a gallop, and the rodeo, in which the branch is thrown every which way, is impossible. But how many rodeo riders do their profession standing up?

By the time the four of you return home, you are tired but happy. No one was hurt, except perhaps the dog that yelped when Danielle got thrown off at a gallop and landed on top of her. But she's wagging her tail now. One thing is for certain, though; you all got pretty dirty. Aunt Debbie's first four words to you are: "Hi. Have fun? Showers."

THE END

Dave keeps his word. When you state that you would like to explore around the rabbit burrows, he heads home. The dog follows him. "It doesn't really matter," Danielle shrugs. "I don't want to kill a rabbit; I just want to explore."

All around are tall twiggy bushes overgrown with tall, dry grass. "The rabbit burrows are under these thickets," Danielle informs you. "And that," she points toward her feet, "must be a rabbit trap." A small bush has been stripped of leaves and branches. Someone has tied a piece of string to the top of the bare stalk. The other end of the string is tied in a lasso loop with a slipknot. The lasso is propped slightly above the ground in a circular shape by sticks and rocks. The lasso knot is pegged to the ground with a small stick. The peg is tied to a piece of carrot, which someone has placed in the center of the circle. "So if the rabbit wants the carrot, it has to enter the circle of string. If it pulls on the carrot, the peg comes out, the little tree snaps up and the lasso tightens around whatever is inside. A rabbit could gnaw the string through, though, if the person didn't check the traps often." You both continue walking.

You arrive at a path through the woods. A group of girls comes walking down it, chattering noisily. They have buckets of laundry and dishes. They laugh upon seeing you and Danielle, exchange a few words with her and then keep on down the path talking just as noisily as before. "I've been down this path before," Danielle chuckles. "It was before I could speak Kiswahili well. Our family went to the pastor's house for an Easter lunch, along with the rest of the church. Dave had gone off somewhere with the boys. I found the girls out back, doing what girls do when on holiday. Talking. I couldn't speak much, but they included me in their group. We played tic-tac-toe. I was really happy to have finally found some friends who were girls. Before I met those girls, the only other kids I ever saw were the boys who came to play with Dave.

"A little while into my time with the girls, they all got up to leave. The food wouldn't be ready for another hour and a half. I didn't know where they were all going, but I wanted to go too. They were a little surprised when I asked if I could come along, but they said, 'Yes.' We all headed down this path through the brush. That's when I found out where this path leads." She laughs and heads into the brush on the other side of the path.

"So, where does it lead?" you ask impatiently.

"Well, that *was* the question," Danielle continues, prolonging the suspense. "When we left the brush, I saw that we were headed for the lake. Of course I got confused. They had no buckets to fill with water, no dishes to wash and no clothes to wash, except the ones that they were wearing. Then it hit me. We were heading for the women's bathing area! Suddenly the girls were stripping all around me. They asked me if I was going to come in with them. I told them the truth; 'My parents won't allow me to go in the water because of stomach bugs,' was the best I could do, Kiswahili-wise. They sympathized with me for having such killjoy parents. At that particular moment, I couldn't have been more thankful for my parents' rule! I said good-bye, left and ran all the way up that path to the pastor's house. I sat with my parents until lunch was served."

A weasel darts across the ground in your path. "Well," Danielle comments, "at least we saw one animal out here. And you got to hear one of my most embarrassing moments. Let's head back home. Besides, the sun is beginning to go down, and we need to get showers before dinner." She looks down at her sooty arms. "Nothing like rolling down an ashy sand-pit for getting dirty."

THE END

"I guess we can just go explore the rabbit burrows another day."

Danielle is okay with your decision but miffed at Dave. Getting home is harder than you thought it would be. You are now crawling along dog paths under low spreading trees. A "dog path," as Danielle and Dave call it, is a cleared path made by the dogs that often walk there. As a result, these paths are clear and navigable but only high enough for a dog. On your hands and knees, the three of you can travel fairly quickly. "Stop, shhhhh!" Dave commands from the front of the train. You and Danielle stop crushing through the dry leaves, and Simba even stops moving. "Listen!" Far ahead you can here the hum of two or three voices as well as the breaking of sticks and the cautious chop of a *panga*, a large African all-purpose knife.

"*Kuni* robbers!" Danielle breathes.

"Don't let them know we're here!" Dave whispers. "Let's try to get home without them noticing us. If you have to make noise, try to time it with the chops and with their speech."

Getting home is a very slow process from this point on. Dave leads you in a wide circle around the voices. Finally you reach a human path and are able to run silently. "We've got to make it home before they get away!" You reach the missionaries' sandy driveway and from there run to the house. Aunt Debbie meets you. Upon hearing the news, she goes over and gets their African neighbor next door. Once she and the neighbor are making their way stealthily toward the voices, Danielle gives you a quick explanation of what is going on.

"*Kuni* is the African word for firewood. The church owns the land behind our house. It is protected land. People are not allowed to chop down its trees or to gather its dead wood. This whole area of Tanzania used to be a huge forest. Now, because of deforestation for firewood, everywhere except the church land is almost completely devoid of trees. People like to try to sneak into the church land to cut firewood. When we hear *kuni* robbers, we try to catch them in the act. Our African neighbor is a tree farmer. He cares about the trees as much as we do, and he is better at convincing people not to come back."

Aunt Debbie is coming back into the yard. "We caught two young women gathering *kuni*."

"I'm sure that there was a man with them a while back," Dave says.

"He got away." Aunt Debbie continues, "They had the usual excuse, 'We are visitors here, and we didn't know. Our relatives sent us here to get firewood and didn't tell us that it was forbidden.' Since both our family and our neighbor's family only moved here a few years back, we can't tell if they are visitors or not. He recommended that we cane them, so that they would be sure not to forget the law. They started crying real tears and begged him not to beat them, saying that they would remember. He said that he would only cane them if they ever forgot again. They promised that they never would. I think that they were telling the truth." Aunt Debbie shakes her head. "I still think that it's a losing battle. Other areas of Tanzania are completely deforested. This area is well on its way if nothing changes."

THE END

You decide to try the monkey-escape. After all, you're only going to hang and then drop about five feet. How bad can it be? Bravely you sit on the starting branch and firmly grab the one in front of you. From there you just slide off. Then you look down. Your feet may only be about five feet above the ground, but your eyes are higher. "Let go!" Danielle coaxes.

"Don't forget to bend your knees when you land!" says Dave. You tell your hands to let go and feel yourself falling. You relax on impact and fall backwards. That was easy! Dave and Danielle seem proud that you were willing to try the monkey-escape even if it was easy for you but are also anxious to get going. Following the sound of Simba's barks, the three of you slowly begin weaving your way around vines and thorn bushes once again.

(Go to page 162.)

You give a quick explanation for your choice not to use the monkey-escape. "I think that with all the time that I would have to take to convince myself to hang from the branch and then let go of it, it would be much faster for all of us if I just climbed down this tree." Danielle and Dave accept your reasoning and wait while you come down. By the time you reach the ground, the barks have become more faint and spread out. "It sounds like she's getting tired." Dave looks a bit concerned for a moment.

(Go to page 162.)

"When we get there, we need to be careful. We don't know what she's barking at." As always, Dave is ready with a word of caution. Simba's barks are getting louder. You finally catch sight of her up ahead. You have left the jungle and have entered "the woods," an area of fewer large trees and less shade than the jungle but considerably more than the brush. Simba is jumping at a short tree, obviously trying to reach something just barely out of her reach. She wags her tail at the sight of you three, as if she is happy that assistance has arrived. She then points to a branch with her nose and waits while Danielle goes to examine it. Danielle stands on tiptoe. "Kittens!" she squeals. Dave rolls his eyes at her squeaky voice and goes to look himself.

"Danny has this love of baby animals...."

"Any animals," Danielle clarifies.

"Not monitor lizards," Dave reminds her.

"Well, yeah," she agrees. "Ah, look at de cute liddle tings! They don't seem to be domesticated kittens."

Dave comes in for a closer look. "I think those are genet cat kittens. They're long and skinny like them."

"And definitely wild! That one's hissing at me. It's okay, you liddle…Ahhhhh!" Simba saw her chance and didn't miss it. With one foot on Danielle for support, she rears up to her full height and hits the side of the nest with her other foot as Danielle slips off to the side. The rim of the makeshift nest is torn, and one of the little kittens comes tumbling out. Like a slow motion picture, Dave grabs the kitten with his left hand and sticks his right hand toward the drooling jaws of the dog just about to get a quick bite to eat. Luckily his hand goes below her teeth, and the force of his arm on her front pushes her back long enough for him to hand the kitten to Danielle to put back in the broken nest. She jumps up and steadies the nest itself to try to keep the snarling, snapping little kittens from falling out. Dave grabs the dog and Danielle steps away from the nest.

"What am I, the savior of baby animals?" Dave looks shocked at himself. "Two in one day? This is ridiculous!"

"I helped too," Danielle reminds him. Then she giggles and brushes some dirt out of the scratch on his back.

"Ouch!" Dave winces slightly.

"Wounded in the act of heroism," Danielle sighs.

"By the baby's mother!" Dave grimaces. "Let's get out of here before the mother genet cat shows up!"

After checking once again to make sure that the genet cat nest on the tree branch is secure, Danielle is ready to leave. "By the way," she asks Dave, "when you rescued the baby bird, are you sure you put it back in the right nest? Maybe that bird wasn't its mother, just another bird trying to keep you from adding an unwanted resident into her humble abode."

"Of course I'm sure! There were other little birds in the nest just like it."

"Sounds good. Just checking," Danielle grins.

Dave rolls his eyes again, as if to say, "Sisters!" Then he makes Danielle an offer.

"If you want, we could go by there on the way back, so that you could check it out."

"No, thank you!" Danielle eyes the scratch on his arm. The four of you, dog included, return home.

THE END

GLOSSARY

Bazungu: the Wasukuma version of the word "wazungu"

chai: tea with milk

Chiro: night (Kizinza word **omuchiro**); also the name of the missionaries' cat

hodi (*hoe-dee*): a word spoken by visitors entering the yard to inform their hosts that they have arrived

jiko (*jee-koe*): a small, hourglass-shaped oven filled with charcoal

karibu: welcome

kenge (*kain-gay*): a monitor lizard

Kiswahili: the national language of Tanzania

Kizinza (*key-zin-zah*): the language of the Wazinza people

kuni (*coo-knee*): firewood

Luo: a Kenyan tribe; many are migratory fishermen

maji: water

marahaba: do it a few times

Mzinza: a member of the tribal group Wazinza

ndege (*n-day-gay*): a bird

nita kuchapa: I will spank you

panga (*pawn-gah*): a large multi-purpose knife. Is used to cut anything from meat to firewood

sana: very much

shikamo: the local greeting from a younger to any older person; "I grab your feet."
Simba: lion; also the name of the missionaries' dog
soko: an African marketplace
sungura: a rabbit
Wasukuma: the largest tribal group in Tanzania (approximately 2.5 million); Kahunda is a Wasukuma village
Wazinza: the tribal group that speaks the language Kizinza
Wazungu: Western people or white people

WHAT'S WYCLIFFE

The family you read about in this book may not be real, but they represent thousands of people who are a part of the Wycliffe team. What's Wycliffe? It's an organization of people from all over the world. What do they have in common? They all love God and value the Bible as God's Word. *And* they want everyone, everywhere, to know about God's love and be able to hear God's Word in their own language.

More than 6,800 languages are spoken in the world. Still about 3,000 language groups don't have the Bible in their language. That means hundreds of millions of people have no way to hear God speak their language! How can they learn about Him? How can they have churches that teach the Word of God?

A young man named Cameron Townsend asked those questions more than 70 years ago. He was trying to give Spanish Bibles to people in Central America and realized that many of the people didn't even understand Spanish. All those languages without a Bible! Townsend was determined to do something about it. Through prayer and partnership, he started a school (SIL) and a mission organization (Wycliffe) to train people to do Bible translation and help get God's Word to the whole world.

Today about 5,000 people from all over the world are a part of Wycliffe. Thousands of other people are involved, working in partnership so everyone can have God's Word in the language they understand best. A few years ago a lot of these partners met together and agreed to pursue Vision 2025. The goal of the Vision is to see Bible translation in progress for every language group that needs it by 2025.

It's a vision for all of God's people, young and old! People all over the world are praying and working together. Some people pray and give money to help fund Bible translation. Some help on short-term projects; other commit their whole lifetime. Whole churches are getting involved: youth groups, women's groups, retired people. There is something for everyone to do! Translators are needed, but you don't have to be a translator to help with Bible translation. There are teachers, computer specialists, graphic designers, office managers....

What's Wycliffe? It's people like you who want everyone to hear God's Word in the language they understand best! Learn more about how you can be involved by going to *www.wycliffe.org*.

COMING SOON

Two New East African Adventures

The Canoeing Safari

The Village Safari

ABOUT THE AUTHOR AND ILLUSTRATOR

Tania Matthews started writing the *East African Adventures* when she was 13 years old. She grew up as a Wycliffe missionary kid in Tanzania, Africa, where her parents served as Bible translators. Storytelling and writing have always been her hobbies. At 7 years old she began dictating stories to her mother to write down. Later she created little illustrated books using cereal boxes for covers. Tania finished high school in Kenya and currently attends the University of Tennessee at Chattanooga.

Judy Rheberg is a retired art teacher living in northeastern Wisconsin with her husband Jim. They spend winters volunteering for Wycliffe Bible Translators in Orlando, Florida. Judy loves animals. She raised sheep to save money for college and once had 10 collie dogs and 20 barn cats as pets. But Judy's all-time favorite animal is the horse. Even after plenty of rough rides and getting bucked off a time or two, she continues to love grooming, riding, reading about and drawing horses of all kinds.